JACK WINTERS' GRIDIRON CHUMS

MARK OVERTON

1st WORLD
LIBRARY
Literary Society

Jack Winters' Gridiron Chums

Mark Overton

© 1st World Library – Literary Society, 2004
PO Box 2211
Fairfield, IA 52556
www.1stworldlibrary.org
First Edition

LCCN: 2004195345

Softcover ISBN: 1-4218-0179-5
Hardcover ISBN: 1-4218-0079-9
eBook ISBN: 1-4218-0279-1

Purchase *"Jack Winters' Gridiron Chums"*
as a traditional bound book at:
www.1stWorldLibrary.org/purchase.asp?ISBN=1-4218-0179-5

1st World Library Literary Society is a nonprofit
organization dedicated to promoting literacy by:

- Creating a free internet library accessible from any
  computer worldwide.
- Hosting writing competitions and offering book
  publishing scholarships.

**Readers interested in supporting literacy
through sponsorship, donations or
membership please contact:
literacy@1stworldlibrary.org
Check us out at: www.1stworldlibrary.ORG
and start downloading free ebooks today.**

Jack Winters' Gridiron Chums
contributed by Tim, Ed & Rodney
in support of
1st World Library Literary Society

CONTENTS

CHAPTER I

GRUELLING FOOTBALL PRACTICE

A shrill whistle sounded over the field where almost two dozen sturdily built boys in their middle 'teens, clad in an astonishing array of old and new football togs, had been struggling furiously.

Instantly the commotion ceased as if by magic at this intimation from the coach, who also acted in practice as referee and umpire combined, that the ball was to be considered "dead."

Some of those who helped to make the pack seemed a bit slow about relieving the one underneath of their weight, for a half-muffled voice oozed out of the disintegrating mass:

"Get off my back, some of you fellows, won't you? What d'ye take me for - a land tortoise?"

Laughing and joking, the remaining ingredients of the pyramid continued to divorce themselves from the heap that at one time had appeared to consist principally of innumerable arms and legs.

Last of all a long-legged boy with a lean, but good-natured face, now streaked with perspiration and dirt, struggled to his feet, and began to feel his lower extremities sympathetically, as though the terrific strain had centered mostly upon that particular part of his anatomy.

But under his arm he still held pugnaciously to the pigskin oval ball. The coach, a rather heavy-set man who limped a little, now came hurrying up. Joe Hooker had once upon a time been quite a noted college athlete until an accident put him "out of the running," as he always explained it.

He worked in one of Chester's big mills, and when a revolution in outdoor sports swept over the hitherto sleepy manufacturing town, Joe Hooker gladly consented to assume the congenial task of acting as coach to the youngsters, being versed in all the intricacies of gilt-edged baseball and football.

It had been very much owing to his excellent work as a severe drill-master that Chester, during the season recently passed, had been able actually to win the deciding game of baseball of the three played against the hitherto invincible Harmony nine.

Mr. Charles Taft, principal owner of the mill in question, was in full sympathy with this newly aroused ambition on the part of the Chester boys to excel in athletic sports. He himself had been a devoted adherent of all such games while in college, and the fascination had never entirely died out of his heart. So he saw to it that Joe Hooker had considerable latitude in the way of afternoons off, in order that the town boys might profit by his advice and coaching.

"A clever run, that, Joel," he now told the bedraggled

boy who had just been downed, after dragging two of his most determined opponents several yards. "The ball still belongs to your side. Another yard, my lad, and you would have made a clean touchdown. A few weeks of hard practice like this and you boys, unless I miss my guess, ought to be able to put old Chester on the gridiron map where she belongs. Now let's go back to the tackle job again, and the dummy. Some of you, I'm sorry to say, try to hurl yourselves through the air like a catapult, when the rules of the game say plainly that a tackle is only fair and square so long as one foot remains in contact with the ground."

So Joe Hooker had been laying down the law to his charges every decent afternoon, when school was out, for going on two weeks now. He seemed to feel very much encouraged over the progress made by a number of the boys.

Already he had weeded out three aspirants for honors on the eleven, who had shown no genuine aptitude for the exciting game where headwork and footwork combined go to bring success.

Others feared the coach had his eagle eye fastened on them, being doubtless conscious-stricken with the knowledge that they were not in their element. Indeed, it was no unusual thing to hear one of these boys say to his mates that he hardly knew whether he cared to try for the squad after all; which admission would serve to let him down gracefully in case his suspicions were later on confirmed.

But there were others who developed wonderfully under the friendly instruction of the one-time star player. Among them, besides the tall chap, Joel

Jackman, might be mentioned a number of boys whose acquaintance the reader of other volumes in this series has already formed.

There was Jack Winters, looked upon as a leader in all sports, and late captain of the baseball nine; it seemed to be already taken for granted that he was bound to be given some position on the gridiron, for Jack seemed to have a wonderful faculty for getting the best out of those who played in strenuous games with him.

Jack Winters was really something of a newcomer in Chester, but he had hardly landed in the old town than something seemed to awaken; for Jack made up his mind it was a shame that, with so much good material floating around loose, Chester could not emulate the example of the neighboring towns of Harmony and Marshall, and do something. There were those who said Jack's coming was to Chester like the cake of yeast set in a pan of dough, for things soon began to happen.

Then there was Toby Hopkins, one of Jack's particular chums, a lively fellow, and a general favorite. Another who bore himself well, and often elicited a word of praise from the coach, was sturdy Steve Mullane, also a chum of the Winters boy. Besides these, favorable mention might also be made of Big Bob Jeffries, who surely would be chosen to play fullback on account of his tremendous staying qualities; Fred Badger, the lively third baseman who had helped so much to win that deciding game from Harmony before a tremendous crowd of people over in the rival town; and several other boys who may be recognized as old acquaintances when the time comes to describe their doings on the gridiron.

It was now well into October.

Already the leaves had begun to turn scarlet and gold on some of the hedges, and even in the forest, where the boys were beginning to go for the early nuts. Early in the mornings there was a decided tang to the air that hinted at frost. Considerable talk was being indulged in whenever a group of boys came together, concerning the prospects for a regular old-fashioned winter, and many hopes along this line were indulged in.

There was a good reason for this, Chester being most favorably situated to afford her young people a chance to enjoy ice sports when the bitter weather came along. Right at her door lay beautiful Lake Constance, several miles across; and the intake at the upper end near the abandoned logging camp was the crooked and picturesque Paradise River, where wonderful vistas opened up with each hundred yards, did any one care to skate up its course for miles.

And with this newly aroused spirit for outdoor sports in the air, also a splendid gymnasium in the course of building where the boys of Chester could enjoy themselves stormy days, and many nights, during the winter, it can be easily understood that a glorious prospect loomed up before them. Why, over in Harmony they were getting decidedly envious of the good luck that had befallen Chester; and all reports agreed that their football squad was working fiercely overtime with the idea of overwhelming utterly all rivals on the gridiron, once the Fall sports opened.

By slow degrees, as he saw best, Joe Hooker was leading his charges along the rugged path; for there is no loyal road to a knowledge of the intricacies of successful football. Constant practice alone will make a player act through intuition, since the plays are so lightning-like that there is never any time to figure out what is to be done; all that must be considered beforehand, and the player be able to decide what the most probable scheme of his opponents is likely to be.

After they had again gone through a series of tackles, using the dangling dummy for the practice, and being shown by old Joe in a spectacular fashion just what was the proper and lawful method of interfering with the man who was supposed to be running with the ball, play was called off for the day.

It was about time, for some of the fellows were panting for breath, owing to the vigorous way in which they had been working. Besides, most of them would need a bath before they could be allowed to sit down at the family table.

"I've been asked by several persons deeply interested in football," Joe Hooker remarked, as they gathered around him for a parting word, some looking anxious, as though they half expected to receive their dismissal then and there, though it was not Joe's way to "rub" it into any one, "what chance we had to meet Harmony with a team that would be a credit to Chester. To all such I give the same answer. There is no reason to despair. We have plenty of promising material, though it will need constant whipping to get it in shape between now and the first game with Marshall. That will be a test. If we down those fighters we can hope to meet Harmony on something like even terms. Tomorrow I shall have to drop out several boys who, I'm sorry to say, do not show the proper qualifications for the rough game; but I want them to understand that we appreciate their offering their services, and we need their backing all the time. Our motto must be 'Everything for Chester!' Now get away with you, and if the day is half-way decent, meet me here tomorrow, prepared to strive harder than ever to hustle for victory."

And with that the boys commenced to start homeward.

CHAPTER II

THE BOY WHO WAS IN TROUBLE

As usually happened, the three inseparables, Jack, Toby and Steve, kept company on the way home. They had much in common, and only that summer the trio had spent a glorious two weeks camping up in the woods of the Pontico Hills country. There were a number of remarkable things connected with that outing, and if the reader has not enjoyed already its perusal, he would do well to secure the preceding volume of this series, and learn just what astonishing feat Jack and his chums carried to success.[Footnote: "Jack Winters' Campmates."]

"I wish both of you could drop over after supper," Toby Hopkins was saying as they trudged along with the air of tired though contented boys. "I've got those plans for our new iceboat nearly finished, with several novel suggestions which I'd like to ask your opinion about before I order the wood to make it in my shop."

"I guess I can run across lots, and spend half an hour with you, Toby," Jack announced; "though I couldn't promise to stay late, because I ought to be doing some of my lessons, you know. This football work after-noons throws everything out of gear."

Mark Overton

"Sorry to say I'll have to beg off this time," said Steve. "Fact is, I've got a date, and couldn't break away very easily. Another time will have to do, Toby. And of course whatever you and Jack decide on goes with me, you understand."

In fact it was almost always that way, such unlimited confidence had both Toby and Steve come to place in Jack Winters. But then he merited all their high esteem, for rarely did things go wrong when Jack's hand was at the helm; he seemed to be one of those fellows whose judgment is right nine times out of ten. Looking back, the Chester lads could begin to understand what a great day it had been for them when Jack came to town, full of ideas which he had imbibed in the lively city where his folks had formerly lived.

"I'm more than ever convinced," Toby went on to say, reflectively, "that we'll be able to put a flier on the ice this coming winter that will have everything beaten a mile. It works out all right in theory anyway."

"The proof of the pudding is in the eating," chuckled Steve, who apparently was not built along quite as sanguine lines as Toby. "But then it'll be a heap of fun to try something new. All the iceboats I've ever seen around here have always been built after the same old model. Nobody ever seemed to think they could be improved on the least bit; and that it was only a matter of the pilot jockeying in order to blanket his rival and win out."

"Joe Hooker seems to be taking considerable stock in what we're doing to build up a machine for gridiron work," mentioned Jack, with a ring of satisfaction in his voice. "I certainly hope we can make things hum around here this Fall. Chester's hour has struck, it seems; and after our baseball victories we ought to be just in time to carry our colors to a sweeping triumph over Harmony and Marshall."

"Some of the boys are showing up splendidly," Steve continued. "I'm a whole lot disappointed, though, in my work today, but I expect to improve, and hope to make the team when the final choice is reached."

"Huh! I guess there isn't much chance of *you* being dropped, Steve," snorted Toby. "I only wish I was as sure of being retained on the honor roll. That run of mine today was as punk a thing as any greenhorn could have attempted. I saw Joe look at me as if he'd like to eat me, and I felt so small I could have crawled into any old rat-hole. But I mean to surprise him yet, see if I don't. I've got the faith to believe I can play quarterback, and I will, I tell you; I'm thinking of it most of the night while I lie awake."

"That kind of grit will take you a long ways, Toby, "said Jack encouragingly. "All of us fall far short of perfection; but Joe is persistent and I've no doubt he already knows just who the members of the team will be, barring accidents, also the substitutes in the bargain."

"We were mighty lucky to have such a dandy coach right at hand," declared Steve; "and Mr. Taft is the best sort of a man to lend him to us so much, at a loss to himself. He contributed heavily to the fund for building the gym, too, I understand."

"Yes," added Jack, "a town that has a few public-spirited citizens of his type is to be congratulated. But here's where I leave you, and hike across lots to my shack, where a nice bath awaits me. See you later, Toby; and sorry you can't join us, Steve."

"Oh! bother," chuckled Toby, maliciously; "he's got something a whole lot better to attend to than just jabbering with his two chums over the lines of a projected iceboat wonder."

Good-natured Steve only laughed in return, though had the gloaming not been settled down so early, the other fellows might have seen his cheeks flaming; for Steve was an exceedingly modest chap, and easily flustered.

Jack Winters reached home, and had his bath in time to come to the table when the supper bell rang. And it goes without saying that his appetite showed no sign of flagging on that occasion, for football work is calculated to put a keen edge on a boy's natural desire for food.

Later on he again set forth, after a hack at his lessons, and turned to make his way across lots along a well-worn path, in this fashion cutting off several corners, and shortening the distance, which is apparently a thing desired by every American lad.

It was about eight when he arrived at the Hopkins domicile, and was let in by Toby himself. The other seemed wildly excited, for the first thing he did was to burst forth with:

"Jack, I've gone and done it, I do believe, this time! Yes, sir, I've struck an idea that promises fairly to revolutionize iceboats. It came to me like a flash, and I'm wild to know what you think about it."

Jack did not enthuse as much as Toby would have liked to see. Truth to tell, Jack had known several of these wonderful "theories" which Toby had conjured up, to fail in coming up to expectation when put to the test; so he did not allow himself to anticipate too much.

Nevertheless when the idea was gone over he admitted that there might really be something in it.

"Perhaps you *have* struck something worth while at last, Toby," he told the other, "and we can work it out by degrees when we get down to actual business. Evidently, you've got an inventive mind, and you needn't despair if a whole lot of your ideas do go by the board. Every inventor has conceived a score of schemes to one he's adopted. Even a failure may be the stepping-stones to success, you know." "That's good of you to say as much, Jack, old chap, when I do think up some of the greatest fool notions ever heard of," acknowledged Toby; "but it's my plan to keep right on, and encourage my brain to work along that groove. I feel it's going to be my forte in life to invent things. I'd rather be known as the man who had lightened the burdens of mankind than to be a famous general who had conquered the world."

Jack did not stay longer than half an hour, but during that time he went over the whole scheme of building the new iceboat in Toby's shop.

"I've got all the specifications down in black and white, you see, Jack," the other said at the door, "as to what we'll need; and now that you've approved, I shall start right in and order the stuff tomorrow. The sooner we get started the better; though I don't suppose we'll really have much spare time to work at it until after

Thanksgiving, and the big game with Harmony is over."

So Jack said goodnight and went out of the front door. Usually he was wont to whistle as he crossed the lots that would serve as a short cut to his own house; but somehow tonight he was busily engaged with his thoughts, and forgot to indulge in this favorite pastime.

It was a moonless night.

The stars shone brightly in the blue dome above, but gave very little light; although it was not really dark anywhere inside the confines of Chester, since the streets were pretty generally illuminated with electricity.

Jack had just started across lots when he made a discovery that aroused his curiosity a little. There was a queer sort of light flickering beyond him. He quickly realized that some person must be walking the same way as he was, and carrying one of those useful little hand-electric torches, which he seemed to be moving this way and that in an erratic fashion.

"Whoever it is," Jack told himself presently, "I do believe he is looking in the grass for something he's lost."

Walking on and a bit faster than the unknown seemed to be going, he soon drew closer, and was able to see that it was a boy who bent over and scrutinized everything upon which the light of his flashlight fell. Once he uttered an exclamation of sudden delight and made a jump forward, only to stop short, and give a doleful grant as though discovering his mistake.

"Oh! how cruel to fool me so," Jack heard him mutter to himself; "only a scrap of waste paper, and I thought I'd found it. Twice now I've gone over the whole lot, and never a trace have I seen. Oh! what shall I do about it? I wish I knew."

Jack by now had recognized the boy as Big Bob Jeffries, the heavy-hitting outfielder of the Chester baseball team, and who was admitted as standing a first-rate chance to be made the sturdy fullback of the new eleven in football.

He was filled with curiosity to know what ailed Big Bob. Something he must have certainly lost which he was now endeavoring to find again, and, if his lament was to be taken at its face value, without much success.

Jack was always ready to lend a helping hand to a comrade in distress. He had proved this on numerous former occasions, so that his first thought was to speak to Big Bob, and ask what was wrong.

At the sound of his voice the other started as though shot, and Jack could see that his face, usually florid and cheery, looked white and drawn. Undoubtedly, then, the Jeffries boy was suffering acutely on account of some carelessness on his own part. Jack suspected that he might have lost some money which he had been carrying home for his mother. As the path was used by a number of persons to "cut corners," it would be next door to a miracle if the lost cash were found again, unless the one who had picked it up proved to be an honest citizen.

"Oh! is that you, Jack?" said Bob, in a trembling tone,

as he turned his flashlight so that its rays fell full upon the other boy. "You certainly did give me an awful jolt, because I didn't dream anybody was so near by. On your way home, I reckon? Well, I suppose I might as well give it up, and go home, too; but I hate to the worst kind, I sure do."

"What's the matter - lost something, Bob?" asked Jack, joining the other.

Bob Jeffries did not answer for a brief time. He was apparently pondering over the matter, and trying to decide in his mind just how far he ought to take Jack into his confidence. Then, as though some sudden impulse urged him to make a clean breast of the facts, he broke out with:

"Jack, to tell you the honest truth, I'm in just a peck of trouble for a fact. You asked me if I lost anything, and you'll think me a bit daffy when I tell you I don't know - I only fear the worst. I'm going to tell you all about it, Jack, because I feel sure you'll never give me away; and maybe yon might even help me."

CHAPTER III

BIG BOB CONFESSES

"Look here, Bob, suppose we adjourn over to my house and have our little talk out in my den. I've got some comfortable chairs there, as you happen to know; and it'll be a heap better than standing here, where people may come along any old time and interrupt us."

That last line of argument seemed to convince Bob, for he immediately agreed.

"The fact is, Jack," he went on to say, "I wouldn't want to have anybody hear what I'm going to tell you now. It certainly is a shame how I've muddled this thing up, and I guess I deserve all I'm getting in the shape of worry. It's going to be a lesson to me, I give you my word on that, Jack."

They were trudging along in company when Big Bob said that. Of course such talk could only excite Jack's natural curiosity still more. He began to understand that whatever the other had been searching for was not his own property, for he was hardly the kind of fellow, inclined to be careless, and free from anxiety, to let such a personal loss bother him greatly.

Presently the pair found themselves in Jack's particular

room, which he, like most boys of the present day, liked to call his "den." It was an odd-shaped room for which there had really been no especial use, and which the boy had fitted up with a stove, chairs, table and bookcases, also covering the walls with college pennants, and all manner of things connected with boys' sports.

Jack closed the door carefully.

"Pick your chair, Bob, and I'll draw up close to you," he said, briskly, as though bent on raising the other's drooping spirits without any delay, just by virtue of his own cheery manner.

Bob looked as though he had lost his last friend. He sighed and then started to tell just what ailed him.

"Seems like I've grown three years older since I suddenly failed to remember about that particular letter father gave me to be sure to post before the afternoon mail went out. I had some others, you see, two of my own, and three that Mom gave me. I can recollect shoving them in the shute one by one; but for the life of me, Jack, I can't say positively that the one going across to England was with the bunch. Oh! it gave me a cold chill when I first had that awful thought I'd lost it on the way. I remembered pulling something out of my pocket when crossing that shortcut path, and that's why I hurried there with my light, hoping to discover it in the grass."

Jack understood what lay back of this. He chanced to know Bob's father was reckoned a very stern man, and that he had grown weary of Bob's customary way of forgetting things, or doing them in a slipshod fashion.

He even knew that Mr. Jeffries had laid down the law to his son, and promised to punish him severely the next time he showed such carelessness.

"It's too bad, Bob, of course it is, but then don't despair yet," Jack told the other boy. "There is always a good chance that you did put that particular letter in the post-office. We'll try to find out if Mr. Dickerson, the postmaster, or his assistant, chanced to notice a letter addressed to England. It must have been of considerable importance, I take it from what you've said already."

"It was just that, Jack; and father impressed its importance on me when he handed it to me stamped, and ready to go. I think it means something big in a business deal of his. Now, in these times when war has gripped nearly the whole world, Uncle Sam with the rest, it's a long wait before you can expect an answer to a letter going abroad, even if the German submarines allow it to reach there. And if I don't find out the truth now, just think of the days and weeks I'll be worrying my head off about that letter! Oh! it makes me just sick to even think of it. I could kick myself with right good pleasure."

Jack realized that this was bound to be the long-needed lesson, by means of which careless Bob would cut loose from his pernicious habit of taking everything free - and - easy. Good might spring from evil, and what now seemed to be a crowing disaster, the boy was likely in later days to look upon as a blessing in disguise.

"If you'd like, Bob," he told his friend, to ease the strain, "I'll see the postmaster in the morning, and without arousing his suspicions find out if he noticed a letter directed to England in the mail yesterday. There are not so many foreign letters going out of Chester these days but what such a thing might happen to catch his eye. If he says there was, of course that'll settle the matter. Even if he didn't happen to notice any such, you mustn't believe it is absolutely certain you dropped it."

"I'd give anything to just know, one way or another. Then I could, if the worst turned out to be true, tell my father, and stand the consequences, for he'd be able to rewrite the letter, you see. But, Jack, it would hit me terribly hard if he has to know what a fool I've been; because he told me if he caught me in any bit of carelessness again this Fall he'd force me to give up all my connection with the football squad, and not even allow me to attend the gym this Winter. Oh! he's in dead earnest this time, and I'm afraid my goose is cooked. It'd almost break my heart to be shut off from connection with my mates in athletic sports, because I'm crazy about such things, you know; it's in the blood, I guess."

Big Bob stretched out his massive arms when saying this, as though to call the attention of his companion to his splendid physique. Indeed, he did look like a boy whom a generous Nature intended to take part in every conceivable manner of athletic sports; no fellow in all Chester was built in quite such a massive mould as Big Bob Jeffries.

"I tell you what let's do," said Jack, immediately afterwards; "I'll get my lantern, and we'll walk back over that path. Possibly the wind may have carried the letter further away than where you looked. How about that, Bob?"

"It's mighty kind of you to take so much trouble for such a stupid comrade, Jack, and let me tell you I appreciate it a heap. Yes, and I'll also get out before dawn in the morning to scour every yard of ground on the way from my house to the post-office. If I could only find that letter I'd be the happiest fellow in Chester, believe me."

So they once more donned their caps, and Jack lighted the lantern he had mentioned. While its rays might not be as strong as the glow of the hand-torch, it was able to cover much more ground at a time; and with its help a white envelope half hidden in the long grass could not escape detection.

Jack could easily understand just what had happened to Big Bob. He had become so "rattled" when that dreadful suspicion first flashed into his brain after supper that for the life of him he found it impossible to say positively one thing or the other. Now he thought he could remember distinctly pushing the important letter through the slot or drop inside the post-office; and immediately afterwards doubts again assailed him, leaving him worse off. after each experience.

If they failed to find the letter, and the postmaster and his assistant had no recollection of having noticed it in cancelling the stamps of the heap that went out with the afternoon mail, then there was no help for it; and poor Bob was doomed to wait day after day, as even weeks went on, always dreading lest each morning was destined to usher in the time when his great crime must come to light, and his punishment begin.

They were soon on the spot, and each with his separate light started to carefully examine the long and tangled grass, now partly dead, that lay on either side of the well-worn path across the lots.

Doubtless Bob's heart still beat high with hope and anticipation; for when Jack on one occasion started to say something he saw the other whirl around as though thrilled with expectations that were immediately doomed to disappointment.

Nothing rewarded their search. Bob might further satisfy himself, and believe he was only doing his duty, by coming out again at peep of dawn and once more covering the ground before giving it up as hopeless; but Jack felt certain nothing would be found. If that letter had dropped from the boy's pocket, then some one must have long since picked it up. He believed he would hear of it if this person, being honest, delivered the letter at the post-office, and told how he had come to find it on the vacant lot.

"Well, it's no use looking any further, I guess, Jack," Big Bob now remarked, in a decidedly dejected tone, after they had gone twice over the entire width of the three lots, and without any success attending their efforts.

"I'm afraid not, Bob," the other admitted with genuine regret, because he felt just as sorry as could be for the poor chap. "I suppose you'll sleep mighty little tonight, for worrying over this thing. Try your level best to follow out all you did when in the post-office. Some little thing may recall to your mind that you certainly did drop that particular letter in the slot."

"I will, Jack, surely I will," Bob told him, vigorously; "but I'm afraid it won't do much good. You see, I've become so mixed up by now, thinking one thing and then another, that no matter what did happen I couldn't honestly say I remembered it. But I still have a little hope you'll hear good news from Mr. Dickerson; or that in the morning it may be handed in at our house, for my dad put his full address on the back flap, I remember that very distinctly. Yes, I'd be willing to stand my gruelling and not whimper if only it turned up."

He walked away looking quite down-hearted, Jack saw. Really he felt very sorry for Big Bob Jeffries. The latter was well liked, having a genial disposition, like nearly all big boys do, the smaller runts being the scrappy ones as a rule, as every one knows who has observed the lads in their play hours, and made any sort of a study of their characteristics.

On another occasion Jack well remembered he had come very nearly losing one of the best players on the baseball nine, when the pitcher, Alec Donohue, appeared exceedingly gloomy, and confessed to Jack that as his father was unable to obtain work in the Chester mills and shops, and had been offered a position over in Harmony, he feared that he would thus become ineligible to pitch for Chester.

But Jack, as so often happened when trouble beset him, took the bull by the horns. He went and saw a gentle-man who could give Mr. Donohue employment, and enlisted his sympathy. It had all ended right, by a place being found for the man who was out of work; and so Alec pitched the great game whereby Harmony's famous team went down to a crushing defeat.

Jack could not but take note of the similar conditions by which Chester was to be threatened with the loss of one of the strongest members of her team.

"Looks as though history liked to repeat itself," Jack mused, as he walked back home after parting company with Big Bob; "only in this case it's the football eleven that's liable to be weakened if Bob's father takes him out; and we never could scare up a fullback equal to him if we raked old Chester with a fine-tooth comb. So I certainly hope it'll all come out right yet, I surely do!"

CHAPTER IV

A FRIEND IN NEED

It lacked only five minutes or so of the school hour on the following morning when Jack Winters, hurrying along, was intercepted by a disturbed looking boy, who had been impatiently awaiting his arrival.

Of course this was none other than Big Bob Jeffries, who had kept aloof from all his customary associates ever since arriving, and had never once taken his eyes off the street along which he knew Jack must come.

He seized hold of the other eagerly. Jack needed no second look to convince him that poor Bob had passed a wretched night. His eyes were red, and there was an expression of mute misery on his usually merry face, that doubtless had induced more than one fellow to ask if he felt ill. No doubt Bob had a stereotyped answer to this sympathetic question, which was to the effect that he was "not feeling himself."

"Oh! I thought you'd never come along, Jack!" he exclaimed, in a voice that quivered with eagerness and anxiety; "though of course I understood that you must be waiting for Mr. Dickerson to be free to talk with you. Tell me what you did, please, Jack?"

"I'm sorry to say I couldn't learn much at the post-office," the other hastened to say, determined not to keep Bob in suspense any longer than could be helped.

"But you did ask about the foreign letters, didn't you, Jack?"

"Yes, I worked that part of it pretty well, and managed to get into a talk about the great difficulty which most foreigners here in this country found in communicating with their old folks abroad. Mr. Dickerson said there was a time when every day he had quite a batch of letters going out to different countries; because you know there are many foreign workers in our mills here, and they were constantly sending money home to their poor folks. But as the war went on, he said, they began to write less and less, because they feared the letters were being held up by the British, or the vessels being sunk with all the mail aboard by the German subs. So he said it was a rare event nowadays for him to cancel the stamps on a foreign letter, though he had one yesterday, he remembered."

"Yesterday, Jack? Oh! what do you mean?"

"But it was to Italy the letter was going," Jack hastened to explain. "Mr. Dickerson said he took particular pains to notice it, because the stamp was put on the wrong end of the envelope. He remembered that Luigi, the bootblack at the railroad station, always insisted on doing this. He also read the address, which was to Luigi's parents in Genoa."

Big Bob's face darkened again.

"Too bad!" he muttered, disconsolately; "why couldn't

that letter he chanced to notice have been my lost one? Hard luck, I must say, all around."

"Then you didn't meet with anything this morning, I take it, Bob?" continued Jack, hardly knowing what to say in order to raise the drooping spirits of his friend.

Big Bob shook his head in the negative.

"Not a thing, Jack," he went on to admit, "though I was really out, and walking up and down that path at peep of day. I couldn't tell you how many times I went over the ground without finding anything. Why, I even remembered which way the breeze was blowing yesterday, and spent most of my time on that particular side of the path. Think of that, will you, Jack; and yet for the life of me I can't positively recollect whether I did drop that letter into the slot along with the rest. I must be getting looney, that's what."

"Well, you've just got to brace up, Bob, and believe it's all right," Jack told him, slapping the other heartily on the shoulder, boy fashion. "As time goes on you'll sort of get used to it; and then some fine day your father will speak of having heard from his correspondent abroad."

"Thank you for trying to bolster up my nerve, Jack It's mighty nice of you in the bargain. I'll need your counsel more than a few times from now on, and I'm right glad I can have some one to go to when I feel so sick with the suspense, All the while I'm waiting and hoping I've got to tremble every time my father speaks to me That's the result of having a guilty conscience you know. I've read about such things before, but this is the first time I've actually had the experience myself."

"Besides," continued Jack, "even if you did mail the letter, that's no assurance it would ever reach the party he wrote to. Many a vessel has gone down before arriving at its destination, a victim to the terrible policy of the Germans with their U-boats. And of course the mail sinks when the boat goes down in the war zone. If your father were wise he would duplicate that letter several times, and in that way make sure one of them had a chance to reach the party abroad."

"Do you know I thought of that myself, Jack!" exclaimed Bob, quickly; "but you see it would never do for me to mention it to him. Why, he'd suspect something lay back of it at once, and ask me the question that I shall be dreading to hear - 'Did you positively mail that letter I gave you?' Jack, sometimes I can see just those words in fiery letters a foot high facing me, even when I close my eyes. It makes me think of the handwriting on the wall that appeared before the eyes of that old worthy, a victorious general, I believe it was, or an ancient king, but which spelled his doom."

"If I knew of anything else I could do to help you, Bob, I'd be happy to try. Now, I do remember reading an account of a gentleman who carried out the very policy of follow-up letters that I was speaking about. He explained how to make sure he reached his corres- pondent across the water he would send a duplicate letter every week for a whole month; and so far he had never failed to connect, although more than one boat carrying his letters went down. Now, perhaps I can find that same newspaper, and give it to you. If you placed it where your father would be apt to pick it up, with the article marked a little, he'd read it, and might act upon it."

"That sounds good to me, Jack. Please look hard, and see if you can run across that paper. It might be the solution of the whole thing. If father wrote again and even a third time I'd lose my guilty fears, because one of his letters would be bound to get across."

"Why, even the possibility of this proving to be a success caused the boy to smile, though he looked almost comical while so doing, because his heart still hung like lead in his breast.

"Well, try and forget it all you can, Bob," Jack went on to say, encouragingly. "I believe I can find that paper, and I'll hunt far and wide for it, I give you my word. If anything else strikes me meanwhile, I'll speak to you about it. If I were you I'd throw myself into the game, and that ought to help you forget your troubles."

"Yes, it's all very good for the time being, Jack," sighed the other, "but say, after the excitement is all over with, and you find yourself nearing the house, and father, the most terrible feeling grips you around your heart. I know I'll have a perfectly terrible month of it, every day seeming to be forty-eight hours long. But it serves me right. After this Bob Jeffries will be a reformed boy, I give you my word for that. Never again can I allow myself to grow careless, and do important things as though I was in a dream. I've awakened at last, Jack."

"Then if that is so, Bob, you're bound to profit by your lesson. It may seem hard, but in the long run it'll pay you many times over. I'll not mention your trouble to either of my chums, though for that matter both Toby and Steve would feel just as sorry as I do. Still, there's no way they could help you, and for your sake and peace of mind I'll keep mum."

Big Bob impulsively clutched Jack's hand, and squeezed it so fiercely that it actually hurt.

"You're a friend worth having, Jack Winters!" he exclaimed, warmly, while his eyes seemed to dim in a strange fashion, though he winked several times to conceal the fact that tears were near. "You put fresh heart into a fellow every time. If you can find that paper with the account of the duplicate letters in it, please let me know, and I'll run over to your house to get it."

"I'll give a big look tonight," Jack assured him; "and I'm almost sure I know just where I saw it. Father never allows papers to be destroyed under a month old, and it'll likely be up in the attic. Depend on me to get it for you, Bob."

Just then the high school bell started to ring, and both lads had to hurry to enter in time. Bob braced up and tried to assume his ordinary look. His pride came to the rescue, for no boy likes to find himself an object of commiseration among his mates. As for Jack, he had to put the entire matter from his mind just then, having other things to occupy his attention.

But every time he chanced to look toward Big Bob during that day's session it would be to find the other staring eagerly toward him; and a peculiar smile would creep across the big fellow's face when he caught

Jack's eye. He was depending on this comrade to extricate him from the pit which his own carelessness had dug for his feet. And Bob was finding how good it was at such a crucial time in his life to have a reliable friend upon whom to lean. Again and again he doubtless told himself how lucky he was to be so favored.

It may be said in passing that Jack did inaugurate a search among the latest pile of papers in the attic that night, and after a thorough hunt actually succeeded in locating the article he had mentioned. His wonderful memory had again served him in good stead, for it turned out to be in the very periodical he had had in mind.

He even went to the trouble to drop over to give Big Bob the paper, marking with, a blue pencil the article just above the item in question. Any one reading this interesting account of something connected with the war must naturally have his attention arrested by the heading just below it, which ran: "How to make sure foreign letters reach their destination in spite of U-boats;" and then went on to tell how the gentleman in question sent out follow-up letters, exact duplicates of the original one.

Bob was intensely interested.

"I can fix it," he assured Jack, "so that this paper will be lying on the floor of the library. I'm glad you had it wrapped around that old sweater you were returning, because if father should ask me about it I can truthfully say I believe you brought it here in that way, and that I must have dropped it in the library; which would be just like my careless habits of the past, you know, Jack."

Taken altogether Jack thought it a pretty good scheme. It might work, too, which would be a fine thing for everyone concerned; since Mr. Jeffries would be sure of having his letter reach its destination, and poor Bob could be relieved of at least a portion of the load that was weighing on his mind.

When Jack left Bob after a short stay, he saw that fresh hope had already taken hold of the other's heart. It had been the fact that he did not know which way to turn in order to try to remedy his mistake that had been the chief cause for the boy's desperation. Now that there was at least a little chance of the ugly affair coming out all right, Bob was beginning to pluck up fresh courage.

CHAPTER V

A MESSAGE FROM MARSHALL

"What does this mean, Phil Parker? Why are you sitting here and watching the boys get the right dope from Joe Hooker out there on the field? I thought you were sure to land a tackle job."

The speaker, a student who wore glasses, and therefore could have no hope of taking part in such a rough game as football, slapped a fellow on the back who was wearing the blue and white sweater of a Chester athlete.

Phil Parker, who had done yeoman service as left fielder on the baseball nine the preceding summer, laughed as he went on to reply.

"Oh! the fortunes of war, Doc. I chanced to be one of those who didn't come up to the scratch with old Joe. And I want to say right now he was right when he made up his mind I wasn't fast enough for his team. I hurt my leg a month ago, and it's never been quite as strong since. I've been expecting to hear something drop, and now it's come I'm actually relieved. The strain is over, and I can root for our team with the rest from the side lines."

"You're the right sort, Phil, I must say," the other student continued, warmly. "With you it's a question of Chester first, last, and all the time. Personal matters ought never to have any part in such things. Every boy ought to be ready and willing to sacrifice himself for the good of the team. That's what I heard Jack telling Archie Frazer, who's also been dropped; but his Scotch blood seemed to be up, and he looked as if he had a personal grievance against old Joe for letting him go."

But the wisdom of the coach weeding out the weak brothers was already beginning to bear fruit. Anyone who knew football could easily see that there was a distinct gain in the general work. It is just as happens in a convoy of vessels trying to slip past waiting submarines; the fastest has to hold up for the slowest, and in consequence much valuable time is lost. It has even been figured that this loss of time amounts to fifty per cent in all.

A new fire and ambition seemed to possess the players on this afternoon. They appeared to adapt themselves to the conditions much more readily than at any time in the past It might be the steady work of the coach was beginning to make itself shown; and that the boys who remained, under the belief that they now had a good chance of becoming members of the fighting eleven, were induced to throw themselves into the battle with fresh vigor.

Joe Hooker encouraged them constantly. His was a policy of this kind, whereas some coaches think it expedient constantly to keep telling their charges that they are unusually dull, and will never make themselves a fighting force; which is apt to discourage fellows, and fail to bring out all that is in them. Joe believed that enthusiasm and a firm belief in themselves would in the end serve best.

Another thing Joe did, which was to let down the unfortunate ones who must be dropped as easily as he could. He talked to them all like a father, and tried to impress it upon their minds that while Chester might not be able to utilize their services that season, there was another time coming. Besides, he endeavored to arouse their pride in connection with the home town, and beg them to do everything in their power to assist in encouraging those who were finally selected to battle on the gridiron for supremacy.

Outside of Archie Frazer no one had shown any ill feeling about the matter; but all tried to take it as the fortunes of war. Jack himself had made up his mind to have a heart-to-heart talk with Archie, to try to win him over. They needed all the backing possible in order to bring success. When there is any bitterness in the hearts of some of those who ought to be shouting themselves hoarse for the home team, it always hurts.

Jack at one time, when resting, and giving another fellow a chance to get in the game, suddenly discovered a strange face amidst the crowd that had gathered to watch the practice. He looked closer, and then remembered where he had seen the boy before.

"Tell me, Stanley," he said to one of the fellows close by, "isn't that Horace Bushnell, from Marshall? I seem to remember him playing on their team when we took that game from them last summer."

"That's right, Jack, Horace it is," came the reply. "He played on third, you may remember, and made some

Mark Overton

rattling good stops in the bargain, that were ticketed for clean singles or even doubles. I was speaking with him a bit ago. He says he's just dropped over to see what's going on in old Chester, once asleep, but suddenly resurrected since you came to town. You'll find Horace a pretty decent sort of fellow, and built along the right lines too."

Jack sauntered over to where the boy was standing watching the exciting melee just then taking place out there on the field, with old Joe Hooker dancing and limping around like mad, shouting directions, or blowing his referee's whistle to indicate that the ball was dead, and that a fresh start must be made.

"Hello! Bushnell!" said Jack, extending his hand with that Free Masonry that always exists among boys. "I thought I recognized you, and asked if you didn't come from Marshall way. Took a notion to see how we were getting along over here, did you? Well, we're making progress, I suppose, but only for our luck in having such a cracker-jack of a coach I'm afraid Chester wouldn't have much show on the gridiron this season; because most of the boys were as green as grass at the finer points of the game."

"He certainly is a dandy coach, all right," asserted the Marshall boy, shaking hands cordially. "I wish we had one half as good as old Joe Hooker. If you fellows make a dent in the game this season you'll owe it all to him. I've just been watching how he works, and it's simply grand. I understand that Harmony is putting in extra licks too this year, being afraid Marshall will down her team. So altogether it looks as if we'll have a pretty lively session."

"I don't suppose, Bushnell, that either Marshall or Harmony has much fear of Chester taking their scalps this year?" laughed Jack.

"Well, you never can tell what may happen in football, until you've tested the mettle of your antagonist," the other sagely replied. "Anything is liable to come along the pike. But as a rule the veterans in the business are those who count; and we take it that few of the Chester fellows have ever been in a real scrimmage; so we expect they'll have a heap to learn. Still, with that veteran coach drilling it in day after day wonders may happen. You've got several weeks for practice before the game with Marshall comes off. If you fellows keep on improving as you're doing now, I can see a jolly struggle taking place, and the result may surprise some folks I know."

"It's nice of you being interested enough in our work to drop in and watch us, and I mean that too, Bushnell," said Jack.

"Well, of course I wouldn't think of coming across later on, when you'll be practicing your signal stunts, and different mass plays," hastily remarked the other, coloring a bit with embarrassment. "If Marshall does carry off that game I want to see it won on merit, not trickery. Football isn't a game where such things should be tolerated. Once a chap from Harmony was discovered watching our late signal work. He had a pair of field-glasses, and was perched on top of an old ruined chimney, from which place he had a fine view of the field. We didn't do a thing about it, only changed our signals in secret. Well, believe me, that came near losing the game for Harmony. They took it for granted that we would play the original signals, and in trying to cut us off left an opening that gave us a chance for our first touchdown. And it was only after the hardest kind of savage work that they were able eventually to lay us out cold, but only by a score of seven to nine."

"That was playing dirty ball," said Jack, indignantly. "I hope they won't repeat that thing this year."

"I hardly think so," the Marshall boy hastily went on to say. "Their paper gave them a rough deal over it, and told them they deserved to lose every game where they placed any dependence on trickery, rather than true merit. Some of the Harmony fellows were heartily ashamed of it all, and came over to apologize after they learned about it. I don't believe such a thing can ever happen again around these parts. You weren't here then, Winters, which accounts for your not knowing about it. But what message shall I take to our fellows from you, as I understand you have been selected to be captain of the eleven?"

"Only this, Bushnell," said Jack, impressively. "We're going into this thing with all our vim. We mean to wrest a victory from Marshall by fair means, if it can be done. If luck is against us we'll be the first to congratulate you fellows over your success; and then get ready to give Harmony the best there is in us. We believe in clean ball, and you never need be afraid that a Chester fellow would be guilty of spying on your team when practicing signal work. If one did we'd refuse to take advantage of his knowledge, and warn you that such a thing had occurred."

"That's the right kind of talk, Jack Winters!" exclaimed the other, effusively. "It's just what true sportsmanship means. Every tub must stand on its own bottom, and may the best team win! My comrades will be glad to get a message like that from Chester; and if such a thing should happen as your team beating us to a frazzle, why, you'll not find us poor losers. We'll give you a cheer that'll do a lot to make you buck up against that terrible Harmony crowd."

"I understand," continued Jack, "that you've strengthened your team considerably this season."

"Yes, that's the only thing we've got to counterbalance your possession of such a great coach. We chanced to pick up several star players this year, fellows who moved to Marshall lately, and who have played on other teams before. Two of them are grand goal kickers, and may give you the surprise of your lives later on. Then we've got a dandy end who is like lightning on his pins; and once he gets the ball he can bewilder the best of them by his ducking and doubling. Well, enough for the present. I don't want to discourage you, Winters, but take my word for it, Chester has to go the limit if she hopes to snatch that game from us. We're full of ginger and - say, that was as fine a kick at goal as could be. That big chap is Jeffries, isn't he? I remember his fielding when we played ball last summer; and the way he swatted the pill was a caution. It nearly broke our pitcher's heart. I guess some of your fellows can do stunts? as well as our stars. But I must be going back home, for I ran over on my motorcycle, you see. Wish you all the luck going, Captain Winters; after Marshall, of course!"

Jack rather liked Horace Bushnell. He did not know as yet whether the other was to play on the rival team, but at least he had shown his heart was set on his home town coming out victor in the approaching contest on the gridiron.

At any rate it was a pleasure to know such an honorable fellow was to be an opponent, and that the Marshall boys were so utterly opposed to any form of double-dealing or trickery, in order to win.

CHAPTER VI

JACK AND JOEL INVESTIGATE

So the time passed, and a week, yes, fully ten days more had gone, with the Marshall game only a few more days away. All this while the coach had kept at his constant grind, trying to get the eleven so accustomed to the many plays of the game that they could act through instinct rather than reason.

Every boy remembers how difficult it was at first to ride a bicycle, when equilibrium was a thing to be studied; but how after the muscles of the body had grown accustomed to adapting themselves to the slightest motion of the wheel, from that time on it seemed the easiest thing going to do all sorts of stunts while riding.

So with football, where the action must be as quick as a flash. Players who are dull-witted never make any great success in the game, no matter how clever they may appear at some particular feat.

Old Joe Hooker knew this only too well. It had been the reason for his detaching several promising fellows who could never understand why they were given the "Indian sign" and dropped; but the fact was Joe had found they could not break themselves of the habit of stopping just a brief space of time as if to consider, before making a play; and that second or two lost, he knew, might account for the game.

It had now reached the critical point where they were practicing signals. While doing this it was deemed wise that they should get away from all spectators; not that they feared any Chester boy would be so mean as to betray their codes to the enemy, or that either Marshall or Harmony would descend to taking advantage of such underhand treachery; but then it was the ethics of the game that such things should be kept to the players themselves.

So on this particular Wednesday afternoon, besides the eleven in the field there were only a dozen select fellows on hand, and all of them really held places as substitutes of one sort or another. Some of them were likely to be called into action in case a fellow got hurt, and had to be taken out; so they were just as vitally interested in this secret work as any one could be.

During the course of the afternoon they would all be given an opportunity to take part in the play going on, so as to become used to it.

As the great day approached everyone seemed to be more filled with ginger than at any time in the past. Coach Hooker was racing this way and that, calling, adjuring, scolding mildly at times, but always with an eye singly to the advantage of the Chester interests. If the team did not pull off a victory with Marshall few there would be to say it was any fault of old Joe.

Jack had been in the melee for quite some time now, and was giving way to a substitute who seemed eager to get in the game. Joining the group over at one side Jack fell into conversation with some of his mates.

As he stood there he continued to follow the excited actions of the bunch out on the field. The counting could be plainly heard, and then would come the lightning-like play as the ball was put in motion; fellows leaped into action, each with a definite aim in view. Then Joe would call them back, to tell them where they fell short, and could improve on the play.

"Old Joe seems to see everything that goes on, just as if he had a dozen eyes in his head," remarked Joel Jackman, who was also allowing a sub to take his place in the line-up.

"Well, that's what makes him the clever coach he is," Jack told him. "In his way he's like the old orchestra leader, Theodore Thomas. I've heard it said that when his orchestra of a hundred and twenty pieces was practicing some big movement by one of the great composers, Mr. Thomas would suddenly stop the music, and scold one player in particular. His wonderful ear had caught a note that was imperfect, and he had been able to pick out the chap who was guilty. Well, that's the way with our Joe; only in this case it's his eye that is highly educated, instead of his ear."

Joel moved aside with Jack.

"Listen to me, Jack," he went on to say, impressively. "Some of the boys here chanced to mention the fact that last year a Harmony fellow tried to steal the signals of Marshall, and in fact did so; but the other fellows discovered him watching the play from a tree

Mark Overton

or some place, and they just changed their code of signals after he had been scared away. Now, Jack, don't look surprised when I tell you I've got a sneaking notion we're being spied on right at this very minute!"

Jack saw that Joel was not joking, and he looked serious.

"What makes you say that?" he inquired, immediately.

"I haven't mentioned anything about the matter to the fellows; in fact, I only got on to the game about the time you dropped in. Just turn to the right a little, will you, Jack. I'm not pointing, because it would tell the skunk we knew about his being there. See that bunch of trees over yonder, do you? Pretty thick, all right, and offering a splendid asylum to any chap who might want to watch what we were doing out in the open field. He's up in the largest tree, that's right."

"Did you see him then, Joel?" asked the other, after staring for a brief interval in the direction indicated, without noticing any incriminating evidence.

"Well, no, I can't say that I did, though it seems to me there is something like a bunch in that crotch about ten feet from the ground; but the branches sort of screen it. But, Jack, I saw the sun flash from the lens of a pair of glasses, not only once but several times."

Jack continued to watch. This sounded like serious business, and he began to feel something like indignation surging up within him. If there was anything Jack Winters despised it was underhand work. Straight and aboveboard himself he was unable to conceive how any fellow could so demean himself as to wish to win by trickery.

"There, didn't you see that flash then, Jack?" whispered Joel, eagerly, a short time later on.

"I certainly did," replied the other, between his set teeth.

"Don't you agree with me that there's some one hidden in that same big tree, and watching us through means of powerful glasses?" continued Joel.

"I must say it does look a good deal that way," he was assured.

"Well, what's the answer, Jack? Are we going to stand for such dirty business? Of course he can't exactly catch the signals from over there, unless he's got some way of accentuating his hearing. But he can see the work that's being repeated over and over again, and in that way learn what our play is. It's a burning shame, that's all I can say. I'd just like to take half a dozen fellows and capture that spy. We would duck him in the river, and make him sorry he ever took a notion to peek on us. I heard that Bushnell chap from Marshall was over one day some time ago."

"You can depend on it this spy isn't Horace Bushnell," Jack hastened to assure his companion. "I talked things over with him at the time, and found him a boy after my own heart, who despises trickery."

"But can't we do something about it to let him know he's discovered, and had better chase himself off?" pleaded Joel.

"I'm thinking of a way in which we might at least learn the truth," said the other, thoughtfully. "We've been going over to the little spring to the left for water. Once we get there it would be easy to slip around, for it happens there's plenty of good cover, I notice. In that way we could surprise the fellow, and catch him in the tree."

Joel showed considerable eagerness to try the plan of campaign.

"Let's be starting across for a drink, then, Jack," he urged, and accordingly they set forth.

No one paid any attention to them, because from time to time some of the boys would head toward the spring, when the water in the bucket lost its freshness, and in their heated condition they panted for a cold drink. Jack and Joel both had their heavy wool sweaters on, so they took no chances of catching cold after their recent energetic exercise.

They stopped at the spring, where there was a gourd that could be used for dipping up the refreshing water, and each of them took a drink.

"There, he's still working away!" snapped Joel, indignantly; "I caught another flash when he moved his glasses. The sun chances to shine in just the right quarter to make that flash each time. I only hope the skunk will stay there till we can get him, that's all."

Joel looked so extremely pugnacious when saying this that Jack knew he must be making up his mind just what sort of corporeal punishment best fitted the crime of playing the spy on rivals in football, in order to obtain an unfair advantage over them and taking a game by trickery.

"Now, just duck down, and we'll be off," Jack told his companion.

He had sized the situation up correctly, Joel saw. There was excellent cover running around to the patch of trees among which the object of their solicitude was placed. It would be an easy matter for two such agile lads to bend over and cover that short distance, all the while keeping themselves hidden from the eyes of the party perched amidst the dead leaves of that oak.

It was real exciting work, too, for they fully anticipated having some trouble in making the spy come down after they arrived under the tree in which he was so comfortably perched. Perhaps there might be a pair of them, when the situation was likely to be somewhat more strained. Joel even wished now they had asked a couple of the fellows to accompany them, so as to make the capture more certain.

Once or twice they found themselves compelled to make a little detour, because the ground in front was too open, and offered little in the way of a screen; but Jack knew just how to manage, and Joel was quite willing to leave matters in the hands of his associate. Everybody trusted Jack Winters, when a task was to be performed; and it is a great thing for any boy to possess the confidence of his mates in this fashion.

"We're getting mighty close now, Jack," whispered Joel, presently. "I can see the trunk of the big oak all right. It's got limbs pretty near the ground too, so that spy couldn't have had a very hard time of it climbing up. I reckon he must have hit on that particular tree partly on that account."

"Keep quiet, Joel, he might hear you," warned Jack; although truth to tell there was little fear of that, because all the while there came across the field the cries of the workers and the chatter of those who looked on.

A little farther and Jack stopped short. He held up a finger as if to tell Joel not to say anything. But that worthy was crouching there, listening as if petrified, while a look of astonishment bordering on consternation began to hold sway in his face.

The truth of the matter was both boys had caught a series of giggles, and sounds of low laughter, which undoubtedly came from the direction of that particular tree; and what struck them as a staggering fact was that these gurgling noises seemed to be of a girlish character, rather than to proceed from boys.

Then Jack made a gesture with his crooked finger, and both of them again commenced to creep softly along, wondering what effect their coming would have upon the fair watchers perched in the lower crotch of the giant oak with the spreading branches.

CHAPTER VII

STRANGE FRUIT FOR A TREE TO BEAR

"Oh! girls, you just ought to have seen Fred Badger run with the ball then! They all chased after him, but he dodged them like everything. If the boys win that game from Marshall I'm sure Fred's going to have a lot to do with it!"

Joel chuckled at hearing one girl say that, for he recognized the voice of pretty little Mollie Skinner, on whom it was said the Fred mentioned was rather sweet, since he always accompanied her to choir meeting, and when they had a dance out in the country, she invariably went with Fred. "Well, I don't know what Fred Badger has got over Steve Mullane, or Jack Winters, or even Joel Jackman," said another voice, rather cynically, as though the speaker did not wholly subscribe to Mollie's view that Fred stood out as a shining mark above the rest of the bunch of struggling players.

Joel chuckled again. It tickled him to be mentioned at all by one of the fair watchers in the tree, even though with such a doubtful compliment as "even Joel Jackman!" would imply.

"But I'm beginning to get tired of sitting here in this

ridiculous fashion," said a third one, dolefully, "and taking turns at peeking through Mollie's mother's opera-glasses. I wouldn't have come only I felt so much interest in our boys this year. It's their first appearance on the gridiron, and I'm just wild to see them beat that bragging old Harmony. As to Marshall, I just know Chester will put those fellows down where they belong, at the foot of the class, without half trying."

"Neither would I have gone to all this trouble," spoke up the fair and spirited Mollie, "only for that silly letter my friend in Harmony wrote me, saying that it was a foregone conclusion Harmony would sweep the earth this year because their team had been *terribly* strengthened. In fact she gave me to understand that everything, even to the crepe, had been ordered for poor little new beginner Chester. It kept me awake most all last night; and I felt so much excited that I just *had* to get you girls to come out here and see what our gallant boys were doing."

"Yes, but however are we going to get down from here?" sighed the girl who had spoken second, and whose name was Lucy Marsh, while the last of the daring trio Jack knew to be another pretty maid, Adelaide Holliday by name. "I feel afraid to jump from so high a place; and girls can't climb trees and come down like boys do."

"Would you mind if we came up and helped you, girls?" suddenly demanded Jack, as he and his companion showed themselves.

There were alarmed squeals from the three nesting in the crotch of the tree, and this was followed by girlish laughter when they discovered who the newcomers were. It was not only the boys of Chester who liked Jack Winters; for any girl would be proud to be asked for her company by a fellow like Jack, so universally esteemed.

"You've turned the tables on us this time, Jack," said Lucy Marsh, bravely enough. "It's a case of the biters bitten, evidently. We came to spy, and we've been spied on in turn. Well, since you've discovered us in a tree, perhaps you'd better climb up and help a pack of foolish girls back to the solid ground again. I seem to lose my head once I get off the earth."

Accordingly Jack and Joel joined them, and it was no particular effort to help each girl down. When the last had been safely landed, the boys jumped lightly after them.

"You'll excuse our looks, of course, girls," said Joel. "We've been in a scrimmage and are hardly fit for ladies' company; but all the same we're delighted to have been of service to you."

"And so," remarked Jack, turning to Mollie Skinner, who was small but pert, and as pretty as a peach, "you had a boasting letter from some girl over in Harmony, I think I heard you say as we came up. She tried to discourage you, didn't she? All right, Mollie, you just send her back a Roland for an Oliver; give her as good as she sent. Tell her the Chester boys are going to swamp Marshall next Saturday, just to put them in trim for the great game on Thanksgiving morning with poor old Harmony. Twit her with a few reminders of that last baseball game we played, when Chester trailed Harmony's colors in the dust. I guess you can rub it in good and hard, Mollie, if you try."

"And you guess right, too, Jack Winters," snapped the girl, her eyes flashing with spirit. "I'll compose a scathing letter that will give Maude something to think about from now to Thanksgiving. And let me say that I'll be meaning every word of it, too. Why, after what we've seen you boys do in practice I just feel that fellows like Fred, and some of the others of course, in the bargain, just can't be whipped by any old school team that plays. Those are my sentiments, and I don't care who knows them."

"Those Harmony fellows wear the yellow and black of Princeton, you know," spoke up Lucy Marsh, "and love to call themselves the Tigers. They think to frighten their opponents by a great exhibition of rough play, and try to act as if they expected to just walk away with every game."

"That's right for you, Lucy," chipped in Joel, "but those same tactics didn't carry weight last summer. Chester didn't seem to be afraid of being bitten by the tiger, in fact we managed to devour the beast, hide and all; and let me assure you, girls, we can do it again, don't you fear."

"How about that, Jack, do you subscribe to Joel's boast?" demanded the girl, as though she would be ready to place a good deal more dependence on an opinion from the captain of the eleven than from the left tackle.

Joel laughed.

"You're going to the wrong quarter for that kind of

information, Lucy," he went on to say. "Jack's too modest to boast, as everyone knows, though he'll work his head off to win the game."

"I'm not claiming anything!" declared Jack; "and only saying that Chester will have no cause for complaint, no matter whether we win or lose; for every fellow's grimly determined to do his level best. Victories sometimes hinge on small things, and the luck of the game may go against us. But we'll be fighting all the time up to the blowing of the last whistle that tells the time of the fourth period has expired."

"Tell them what Coach Hooker said this very afternoon, Jack?" begged Joel.

"Please do, Jack," the fair Mollie pleaded; while the other two looked so wistful that Jack could not have declined had he wanted to, which was far from the fact.

"Oh! Joe seemed to be especially well pleased with our work today," he remarked, "and told us that taken all in all we made as lively and hustling a lot of youngsters as he had ever had the pleasure of handling. He even went on to say that if we worked as well in the Marshall game we would carry off the prize as sure as two and three make five. And let me tell you, after hearing those inspiring words we played better than ever the next round, and had old Joe beaming with joy. I honestly believe he thinks a heap of our bunch, since it's been weeded out."

"We're all proud of you, just remember that," said Mollie, boldly; "and we do hope you'll be able to make the Marshall boys eat humble pie next Saturday. Why, nearly everybody that's worth knowing at all in Chester is going over to Marshall to give the Chester salute when you come on the field. I chanced to hear Packy McGraw, your cheer captain, drilling his squad; and let me tell you they can give the Chester yell in a way that thrills the blood."

There could be no doubt about Mollie and her two chums being heart and soul for the local team. Jack was glad to see such enthusiasm. It would make himself and the other ten fellows fight all the harder to know that bright eyes were watching every move that was made; while dainty hands clapped until they ached, keeping company with the defiant cries arising wherever Chester girls congregated, in grand-stand or field.

It means a whole lot to a team to feel that their home folks believe in them to the limit. Just as soon as this interest gives signs of waning the best of teams grow careless, and show signs of disintegration. So Jack hoped the girls as well as the boys and grown-ups of the town would be with them all the while, ready with cheering words and praise for good deeds, as well as apologies for mistakes such as the best of players may sometimes make.

So the three girls departed, binding Jack and Joel to a promise not to betray them to the rest of the squad. This promise both boys gladly gave, for no harm had been done; and they knew now just how earnestly the girls of Chester were hoping and praying for their success. It was really an inspiration, to Joel at least.

"There's no use talking, Jack," he was saying, as they started to go around once more to the place of the spring, to avoid exciting any suspicion on the part of their comrades, "we've just *got* to beat Marshall on Saturday. Why, it'd break the hearts of those pretty girls if we failed. I really believe they'd feel it more than any of us would. And that little spitfire Mollie is crazy to rub it into her boastful friend over at Harmony, too. Oh! we've got our job set out before us for a fact, and must sweep the deck each deal."

The rest of the practice caused the boys to forget their recent little adventure for the time being. They worked hard, and won additional praise from old Joe Hooker.

"You're getting better every day, fellows," he told the bunch as they started homeward, chattering like a lot of magpies. "I never was so pleased with the improvement shown; why, it's simply marvelous. If an old football man should watch some of your plays he'd swear you were anything but novices, and vow you'd done plenty of footwork last season. Don't stop, boys! Keep up the good work, and my word for it, your reward is sure to come, for you'll take Marshall into camp on Saturday, barring accidents."

They would have two more afternoons for practice, and then Saturday would dawn with its uncertainties that might not be relieved until the referee had blown his whistle to signify that the time for the game had expired. Whose would be high score when that minute came around was an unknown quantity; and many a Chester lad would have given much to be able to lift the veil of the future just that far. But this was beyond their ken, and they could only possess their souls in patience while hoping for the best.

Those two days would soon pass, and the great time

come when Chester folks could be seen thronging the road leading to Marshall, bent on witnessing the meeting of the rival teams on the gridiron.

How some of the most impatient managed to pull through the intervening time it would be hard to tell. But finally Saturday morning dawned, and the fact that the sun shone from an unclouded sky, while the air was quite nipping, brought joy to thousands of eager hearts in Chester, and doubtless also in Marshall; for both towns were said to be football crazy this year.

CHAPTER VIII

A CALL FOR HELP

"Hello! Jack, I was just thinking of dropping around at your place. Can you spare me a few minutes of your precious time this morning?"

Big Bob Jeffries called this across to the other, down on the main street of Chester. Jack was hurrying along, after finishing the several errands that had taken him into the heart of the shopping district. It was on the great Saturday morning that was to give the town folks their first taste of real football. Everywhere people seemed to be talking about it, and the chances the local team had of pulling off a victory. Jack, being known as the captain of the eleven, and an acknowledged leader among his fellows, was greeted with many an anxious question concerning the condition of the team, and whether he really and truly expected to score a triumph against the hard-playing Marshall crowd.

To all such inquiries the boy had returned a merry answer, simply saying:

"We're going to do our level best, and we have hopes, that's all I can say. Tell you more about it this evening."

When he heard Big Bob calling out this request a look of real concern flashed across Jack's face, the very first that morning. He feared lest the other was about to spring some sort of disagreeable surprise upon him at almost the last hour.

All along he had managed to keep Bob sort of buoyed up with constantly renewed hope that his troubles were sure to end in smoke. But evidently the big fellow had suffered in secret, and was in quite a nervous state of mind.

"Certainly I can, Bob!" he exclaimed, starting to cross over to where the other stood, looking so forlorn that had any observing fellow come along just then and noticed the expression on his face, he might have spread an alarm to the effect that the big fullback was ill, and consequently there would be a weak spot in the line-up that afternoon, as sure as anything.

"I hate ever so much to bother you, Jack, with my personal affairs, just when, of course, you've got your hands full of the coming battle on the gridiron; but I must ease my head or something will burst, I'm feeling that wretched."

"Come along and walk with me," said Jack, promptly. "I am in a little of a hurry, but we can be going in the direction of my house, and take it slowly. Now what's happened, Bob?"

"Happened, Jack? Why, nothing at all, and that's just what's the matter. If only something *did* come along to break up this terrible monotony, I'd welcome it; but every day's like the one before it. I go to bed, and get to sleep all right, but when I wake up along in the early hours, about two or three o'clock, I begin to think, and lie there till dawn comes, just groaning to myself, and trying to make up my mind what I ought to do."

"I'm sorry to hear that, Big Bob, sure I am," said Jack, his voice telling the same thing. "But you say things haven't changed at home. By that I reckon you mean your father hasn't asked you anything about that letter he gave you to mail?"

"Not yet, Jack, but I'm mighty much afraid it's going to come any time now. You see, he must be getting anxious because he's received no answer to his letter, though of course there hasn't been any too much time so far. But my mother is worried on account of *me*. I've almost lost my appetite. The things that used to appeal to me the most I now let pass with barely two helpings. She knows there's something gone wrong; you can always trust a boy's mother for being the first to suspect that, when he gets off his feed."

"Does she say anything to you?" asked Jack, solicitously, for it pained him to see how much Big Bob felt it all.

"Oh! every day she asks me if I'm real sure I'm not sick," came the slow reply. "I always tell her I'm all right; but say, she knows better, Jack. I can't meet her eyes when she looks at me like that. Once she begged me to tell her what had gone wrong with me, whether I was doing poorly at school, even if my report stood to the contrary; but I tried to laugh that off, and told her I'd soon be all right again, after this football game, mebbe."

"I hope you will, Bob, and a lot of us will have a big

load off our minds if only we can come back home this afternoon, singing, and feeling joyous. Of course you never really knew how that little scheme of mine worked, did you?"

"Meaning the idea of putting that marked paper where my dad would be sure to see the item about the man who sent follow-up letters abroad, so as to make certain one of them would get to its destination, in spite of British blockade and German submarines? Why, no, I never found out if father took to the idea or not. I only know he must have seen the paper, because I found it later on his desk in the library, and I left it crumpled up on the floor. He never asked me where it came from, so I didn't have to tell him you had it wrapped around an old sweater you were returning to me. All I'm sure of is that he didn't trust me to mail a second foreign letter. I only wish he had."

"You said he was beginning to look serious, didn't you?" continued Jack.

"Why, yes, and I can just *feel* him watching me when he thinks I'm not looking. He certainly must suspect something, Jack. But the queer part of it all is that lately he's been a heap more gentle with me than I ever knew him to be before."

"I don't quite get the hang of that, Bob."

"Well, you must know that my dad is reckoned a stern man. Folks have always looked on him as what they call austere. He's engaged in a business that keeps his mind away up in the clouds most of the time, and he just can't pay much attention to the small things of life. I heard him tell that once, and I've tried to understand what it really meant, but somehow I couldn't, because my nature is just the opposite, so I guess I must take after my mother's side of the family. I can hardly remember the time when my dad played with me, or seemed at all interested in my childish hopes and fears. It was always Ma to whom I went with my troubles; and Jack, she never failed me. That's what makes it so hard for me now. Only for you to confide in, I don't know what I'd have done."

He seemed on the verge of breaking down at this point. Jack in order to prevent anything like this hastened to ask again:

"Go on, Bob, and tell me just how your father is acting differently nowadays from what he's always done."

"Why, you see," continued the other, with a spasmodic movement of his big frame that might have been caused, Jack suspected, by a half-suppressed sob welling up from his sorely distressed heart, "he's not only been watching me close at times, but twice now he's even asked me something about the football match with Marshall; and last night Ma told me he had said they must surely go over today and watch me play. Oh! Jack, that nearly broke me all up. I felt just like I must throw my arms around my mother's neck, and pour out the whole wretched story of my carelessness."

"But you didn't, I suppose, Bob?"

"No, I managed to blurt out an excuse for hurrying away, though I kind of think she must have seen that there were tears in my eyes, for she called after me; but I didn't dare turn back right then, and pretended not to hear her. Later on I'd managed to get a fresh grip on myself, and even smiled a little, though I tell you that was the most ghastly smile I ever knew, for it was a hollow mockery, Jack."

"But you've held out this far, Bob, and you must pull yourself together so as to go through the game today," Jack went on to say, warmly. "If you failed us our goose would surely be cooked, you know, because the fellow who has been practicing as your understudy at fullback is a mighty poor fish, and Marshall will know it as soon as the first period is over, especially if they push us hard, and he breaks down, as he's pretty sure to do."

"Oh! as to that, Jack, I'm not meaning to give up just now. I've got my mind made up to play savagely today. I want to forget my troubles, and I'll take it out on Marshall. Besides, I'll always be remembering that Ma and Dad will be there seeing no one but their Bobbie; and it might ease my pain if only I could do some half-way decent stunt that would bring out the cheers, and make them glad I was a Jeffries."

"Shake hands on that, Bob. I felt pretty sure you wouldn't fall down at the last minute."

"I guess I've got a little too much pride in myself for that," said the other, trying to look like his old self for once. "But that Thanksgiving game is another question. If this sort of thing keeps on, I'll surely be a nervous wreck by then, and too weak and wobbly to play."

"Oh! don't cross bridges before you come to them, Big Bob," sang out Jack, wishing to inspire the other with fresh confidence. "That's a poor policy, you know, and some fellows are addicted to it. There's another old saying that you might take to heart, and which runs like this: 'Sufficient unto the day is the evil thereof;' which also means that it is foolish to worry, because nine-tenths of the time what we imagine is hanging over our heads never really comes off."

"Well, one thing I'm sure of, Jack, and that is that you're the boss comforter. No matter how badly I'm feeling, only let me get in touch with you, and I seem to draw in new life and hope. I'll never forget all your kindness, you can depend on that, Jack Winters."

"Oh! don't mention it, Bob; you'd do the same for me, or any other fellow, given a chance, because it's in your nature. But let's speak again of your father, for after all he's the central object of the whole thing. You said in the beginning that you feared he was beginning to suspect you, and that from the way he kept watching you when you were reading, you felt as if he might up and say something about that letter?"

"Yes, sometimes that gives me a cold chill; and then again I'm puzzled to know why he's taken to being so much kinder than usual. Why, honestly, Jack, just last night he even asked me if my old skates were still good for this season's use, or would I like to have a pair like those he'd noticed in the window down at Higgins' store. Oh! that nearly broke me all up. I felt as if I wanted to throw myself down on my knees before Mm, and say that I didn't deserve new skates, or anything like that this year, because I was a wretched, careless boy, who had done something wicked. But somehow I managed to stammer out that I guessed my old ones were going to be good enough for one more season, though, Jack, they are in bad shape; but then it would have made me feel worse than ever if I'd accepted his offer, after failing him when he trusted me."

Of course Jack knew that Big Bob was making a mountain out of molehills, but he could readily understand how that came. The big fellow was extremely sensitive, and the possible enormity of his offense kept standing out before him all the time and constantly growing in dimensions.

What he said about his father made Jack secretly smile. It was about time, he told himself, that a reserved man like Mr. Jeffries woke up, and began to take more interest in his children, and not leave it all to his good wife. And in the end possibly this affair might work out for the good of all concerned, the father as well as the son. Meanwhile, Big Bob must be encouraged to hold on for a time longer, until they could know the actual state of affairs.

CHAPTER IX

HEADED FOR THE FIELD OF BATTLE

Big Bob was already looking better, after what had passed between Jack and himself. Although time counted with the captain of the Chester eleven just then, as he had a number of things he wished to do before noon, he felt that he could well afford to stand by Bob a little longer, and get him to feeling more cheerful.

Football games often depend on small things that might seem trifles to those who do not know that the condition of mind as well as of body, on the part of every member of the squad, has much to do with ultimate success or failure. Therefore, as it might turn out that victory would depend on some play on the part of the fullback, Jack was earnestly desirous of arousing all the ambition he could in Bob's heart.

"Now, see here, Big Bob," he went on to say, as they sauntered along, Jack occasionally waving a hand affably to some boy who called out to him across the street, "I wouldn't think any more than I could help about your father's actions. Because of your guilty conscience you can see only suspicion in his watching you so closely, but I'm able to view it from a different angle." "Tell me what you mean, please, Jack?"

Mark Overton

"It strikes me this way," the other complied. "Your father has just begun to realize how much you and the other children mean to him. I think he has had his eyes opened to this in some way, and that in the future you'll find him changed. Then it would be only natural for your mother to confide her fears concerning your health to her husband. That accounts for his watching you when he thinks you're not noticing. He wonders if you are really sick, and won't own up to it for some foolish reason. I wouldn't be surprised if he gets you to drop in and see the doctor, so as to be examined all over. Why, they may even be giving you a *tonic*, Bob, to try and fetch back that lost appetite of yours."

"Do you think so, Jack?" said the other, with a grim smile flickering about his mouth. "Well, I know the very best tonic that could come to me, which would be the news that the letter he wrote had reached its destination abroad. Oh! if only I could learn that, I'd feel like flying, my heart would be so light. And play, why, Jack, if such glorious news came to me right now I'd wake up those Marshall boys this afternoon, believe me. They'd think a *cyclone* had struck the line when I butted up against it. I'd tear everything to pieces, and the whole gang couldn't stop me; for all the world would be bright again, the birds singing, and best of all, I could once more look my father straight in the eye."

"I wish that sort of thing would happen, that's all, Bob," laughed Jack, partly to conceal the fact that he was pretty much shaken up himself by the way Big Bob expressed his state of feelings. "But even if you don't get word about the letter, I'm confident that your position will be well looked after this afternoon."

"You can depend on me, Jack," said the other, simply, for Bob was not given to boasting.

"There is nothing more you want to say to me, is there?" asked Jack, for they had by now arrived in front of his gate.

"I guess not," answered Bob, making a dive for the right hand of his comrade, which happened to be free of bundles, and which he squeezed most heartily. "Thank you a thousand times for giving me so much fresh hope, Jack. I'm going to try once more to believe that the whole nasty business will come out right. See you when we start across for Marshall this afternoon. I've laid out not to eat more than half a ration this noon, because I want to be in fighting trim."

So they parted, with a wave of the hand; and at least Big Bob did have a more contented look on his face than when he first called out to Jack across the main street of Chester, to ask for a little of his time.

Of course there was no attempt made to restrain the members of the team from eating any reasonable amount of food. They did not go in training for days and weeks before a gridiron battle, as is done in all colleges, their diet restricted to certain lines of food best calculated to add to their vigor, without making them loggy. But Joe Hooker had impressed it on their minds that it would be well for them to avoid certain things that might upset their stomachs; and all had bound themselves not to attend any parties, or stay out of bed later than ten o'clock on any night.

Small things like this often have a tremendous influence in deciding a fiercely contested battle on the gridiron. If one man has been indulging in too rich food, so that his digestion is impaired in the least, he has weakened his system; and in case the crisis of the fight chances to fall upon his shoulders, he will possibly be unable to bear the strain as he might had he been in perfect physical shape.

So far as he knew, every fellow was in the pink of condition, Jack was telling himself as lie worked at something up in his den that morning. He had been chiefly concerned about Big Bob; but this last little interview with the fullback gave him renewed confidence. The mere fact that his father had at last mustered up enough interest in boys' sports to promise to attend the game at Marshall that afternoon had in itself inspired Bob to determine to do his family credit, if it came to him to have an active part in the offense, or rather the defense; for that was where his duty generally came in.

"We've got all the show we deserve," Jack told himself, after viewing the situation from every possible angle. "Joe Hooker has taught us all he knows about the game, and he says we are going to do his coaching credit. That means he believes Chester has a fair chance to win. And if every fellow is as determined to crush Marshall under as Big Bob seems, we'll do the trick, that's sure."

Of course Chester labored under a big handicap, in that they knew so little concerning the playing abilities of their opponents. Most of the boys had, of course, attended previous meetings between Harmony and Marshall, since there was so little interest shown in Chester for any sports. They had seen those young gladiators from the rival towns lock horns, and struggle excitedly for supremacy upon the flat gridiron marked stretch of ground, cheering for one or the other side without prejudice, as their fancy chanced to dictate; but that was not like feeling the brunt of a rush, or trying to outgeneral a swiftly running player with the ball, heading for a touchdown. Actual hostilities alone could give them the confidence in themselves which they needed.

"But," Jack went on to assure himself, "after the first period we'll all be on our tiptoes, and ready to show them what we can do. By then we'll have a good grasp on their style of mass play, and what old Joe has taught us will turn to our advantage. However, it's up in the air still, and as much our game as Marshall's. The only thing I know is that we expect to fight with every ounce of strength we've got in us, and never give up till the last whistle blows. No one could ask for more; no boy do more. And I do firmly believe we'll come back home tonight crazy with joy over our first scalp."

Later on, having eaten a light lunch, Jack set out for the rendezvous, clad in his now well-worn suit. Rough usage soon takes the edge off a new set of football togs, for much of the work is done upon the ground. Whether grass stains or dirt marks, it does not matter. Like a sensitive hunter who proceeds to soil a new suit of khaki garments which he has been compelled to buy, lest some one take him for a novice in the shooting line, so those who play football take the keenest pride in their most disreputable clothes. Every stain stands for a possible struggle on the field that may have spelled a crowning event for the participant. So they come to look upon these marks as those of distinction, just as a soldier would the medal he so proudly wears upon his breast.

The boys were gathering when Jack reached the scene, although it would be more than a good hour before the start was to be made. Some of them looked a shade anxious, he was sorry to notice, though really that was to be expected. Jack made it his duty to try to banish this feeling as far as possible, and to imbue everyone with some of the same confidence that was filling his own heart.

As usual, his influence soon began to make itself felt. There were Steve and Toby also who hastened to back him up, realizing what a factor toward success this feeling of firm reliance on their ability to fight their own battles would be certain to prove.

It was not long before a tremendous crowd had gathered. Boys who expected later on to go over to Marshall stopped to take a last look at the eleven, and figure out the "dope" as to whether they looked like winners or "quitters." And in nearly every instance they went away firmly convinced that Jack's team would give Chester no reason to be ashamed. It seemed to be in the air that great things were about to happen for the old town, so newly awakened. Perhaps the pleasing memory of how Jack Winters had led his nine to victory against both Marshall and Harmony during the late baseball season still lingered in their minds, to inspire fresh confidence.

"Well," Doc Speaker remarked, as he sat in a car with his folks, and surveyed the struggling throng gathered to wish the boys the best of luck, "one thing certain, Sis, if anybody can bring Marshall's scalp home tonight it's Jack Winters. No one seems to just know how it comes, but there's a certain magnetism about that fellow that goes clean through the bunch. You know leaders like Napoleon and our own Teddy Roosevelt are born, not made. Jack is built on that plan. Other fellows who have made up their minds to dislike him, as I did at first, soon come under the magic spell of his nature, and end by believing he can do almost anything he tries. And so we are all firm in the belief he'll carry his team to a glorious victory that'll cause those Harmony chaps to sit up and take notice, because of course every last one of them will be on deck today, to pick up points about our style of play, and see if our line shows any yellow spot."

When finally the big carryall, run by a motor, started off, headed down with the eleven players, Joe Hooker, and the numerous substitutes, it did seem as though the town were deserted. Several of the mills had even closed for the day in order to give their hands an opportunity to go across and help cheer for Chester.

The road all the way to Marshall, distant something like ten miles, was filled with all manner of vehicles from a farm wagon and an old-time buggy to the latest thing in seven-passenger cars. And had a stranger chanced to come upon that road he must have wondered what all the travel meant, possibly concluding that some late circus had come to a neighboring town, or else Billy Sunday was holding forth there to immense audiences.

The nearer they drew to Marshall the greater the congestion became. Other roads leading into the town were likewise thronged with pedestrians, and every manner of vehicles. Such a tremendous outpouring of the people, and not young folks alone, either, had never been known before. Seeing such mobs the Chester boys could not help feeling that they must acquit themselves with credit that day or be forever disgraced.

In this grim frame of mind they finally reached the field where the battle of the young gladiators was scheduled to take place, to see a sight that would thrill anyone capable of being moved by such a spectacle.

CHAPTER X

WHEN THE GREAT GAME OPENED

It must be Marshall's great field day, that was evident. Business would be almost suspended while the game was in progress, only the most necessary stores keeping open. The grandstand was already filled to overflowing, newly arrived crowds trying to find seats anywhere they could, but with small success. Those who had the affair in charge must have underestimated the immense throng that would be attracted to the field by the fine Fall weather, and the prospect of a rattling good game.

As usually happens, the Chester crowds kept pretty much together. They could be picked out as a rule by the swirl of waving school colors, for every Chester girl and boy who had journeyed to Marshall to see their team win the game, made sure to carry the favorite combination.

Of course Marshall did likewise, and as this was their home town, they possibly outnumbered the Chester young people two to one. What they lacked in numbers, however, the visitors seemed able to make up for in noise. From time to time songs rang out over the field, that carried the sentiments of the confident Chester girls, over there with the sole purpose of encouraging their team to carry off the prize.

At one place a large number of boys from the other town seemed to be gathered, and there was always something doing in that especial quarter. Seated in the front rank was a lively little chap who carried a tremendous megaphone. This fellow was no other than the redoubtable Packy McGraw, Chester's cheer captain, who had done such yeoman service during the baseball games in leading the pack to hurl defiance at the enemy, and to encourage the home boys in every way possible.

When the humor seized Packy, or some stage in the game made such action desirable, he would leap the barrier, and jumping up and down like a harlequin in front of the bleacher benches, start his cohort into a combined school yell that must make the hot blood leap through the veins of everyone who called Chester his or her home town.

It was really a most inspiring sight, that immense gathering of people, all filled with animation, and a desire to see one or the other of the contesting teams carry the ball to goal and touchdown, until the victory had been won.

The best, of course, was yet to come, when, game being called, every eye would be riveted upon the figures in the arena, crouching like wildcats ready to bound into life in concert.

While the necessary preliminaries were being attended to, and the players were under close surveillance, naturally much of the talk being indulged in was connected with their appearance.

Some seemed to be of the opinion that Marshall looked much stronger in the way of beef and brawn. It was undoubtedly true that, taken as a whole, the home players did outweigh the visitors. This might prove of advantage to them in certain mass plays, where their machine could mow down all opposition through sheer avoirdupois. But, on the other hand, it is not always given to the heaviest team to win. Speed counts for more than heft in many of the fiercest struggles that take place on the gridiron; and a fellow who can run like the wind, and dodge all interference, is more likely to bring his side success than the slower and more stocky individual who lacks this advantage.

Mollie Skinner and her two chums sat there in the front row of the grandstand where they could have an uninterrupted view of everything that took place. They had come over very early, just to secure these splendid seats, sacrificing their customary warm lunch, it seemed, for each of them had brought a "snack" along, which they had calmly devoured while waiting for the crowds to assemble.

They felt amply repaid, however, for they found themselves envied by many who came later, and could not find a vacant seat. From where they sat they could watch the two teams as they stood in clumps and chatted and laughed, doubtless trying to appear quite unconcerned, for they knew how a myriad of critical eyes must be focused on them just then.

"Well, what do you think of the boys now, Mollie?" demanded Lucy Marsh, upon noticing that the little girl with the clever tongue was observing the players critically.

"I tell you what's bothering me," Mollie hastened to say. "It's that Big Bob Jeffries."

"Why, what ails him?" asked Adelaide in turn. "I always thought Bob Jeffries was to be depended on any time he was needed. Remember how he played in those ball games, and with never an error. Yes, and didn't he knock out more than a few dandy two-baggers, with men on bases? Why should you be worried about him, Mollie?"

"Really I don't know," came the puzzling reply; "only I've heard several people say they didn't believe Big Bob could be feeling himself. He's been acting queer lately. Even Fred Badger admitted that to me when I quizzed him, though he hastened to say that so far it hadn't seemed to interfere with his playing, for he kept holding his own right along. But something seems to tell me that if we lose this game today it's going to be through some bungling play on his part."

"Listen, Mollie," said Lucy just then, "don't speak quite so loud, because Bob's father and mother are just back of us, I've discovered."

"Well, that's a queer thing," said Mollie, without even turning to look. "No one ever knew Mr. Jeffries to take the least interest in outdoor sports before. He must have waked up from his Rip Van Winkle sleep, apparently. I even heard that he declined to contribute a dollar to the new gymnasium that some of the town people are building to satisfy the craving of the boys for physical exercise, saying he guessed boys ought to be able to thrive without all those costly adjuncts; that as a boy he had never found the need for anything of the sort, and that he didn't mean to squander his hard-earned money on any such nonsense."

"Well," put in Adelaide Holliday, "whoever told you that must have been poorly informed, or else there has been a sudden revolution in Mr. Jeffries' beliefs; because my father, who is one of the committee to raise funds to pay the first expense of fitting up the new gym, with all sorts of modern appliances, said just last night at supper that he had had a visit from Mr. Jeffries that afternoon, who asked how the subscription list was coming on, and upon learning that there was still a whole lot needed, handed in his check for a cool hundred dollars. He also told him that if they still fell short when settling things up, to call on him for an additional hundred."

"You certainly surprise me, Adelaide," said Mollie, "but I'm glad to hear that Bob's father has waked up at last to understand just what such things mean in a civilized, up-to-date community like Chester. Old things have passed away, it seems, and everybody who has any sense will get on the band wagon before he finds himself lonesome. But that doesn't ease my mind about our big fullback."

"Why, he seems to be just the same as ever to me, looking from here," expostulated Lucy Marsh.

"Yes, that's because of the excitement, and the fact that his folks are present," explained the doubting Mollie. "I saw him wave his hand to his mother just then. All I can say is I hope he'll do himself credit. Jack Winters assured me there wasn't a weak link in the chain, and when I mentioned Big Bob to him he turned a little red, and hastened to say that he would be found doing his duty as he invariably had in the past. But, all the same, I tell you Jack is a little nervous about him; I could read that in his face when he answered my question so hurriedly."

"Oh! look! they're going on the field, girls!" exclaimed Adelaide just then, and all minor matters were allowed to rest while they watched the opposing players run out and start to take their positions.

A tremendous salvo of cheers greeted their appearance on the gridiron, destined to be the battle ground on which they must struggle for supremacy, utilizing every ounce of strength, and backed up with such generalship as their chosen leaders could bring to bear.

They were certainly a fine looking lot of youngsters, and those near and dear to them had a right to feel proud at that moment when the great game was about to open. The cheering died away as though by some prearranged signal; indeed, it is simply astonishing how during the progress of a game the volume of sound will suddenly break out like a hurricane, and then cease almost as abruptly, so that the whistle of the referee may be heard in its piercing intensity.

As the young athletes lined up on the field they stood in the following order:

CHESTER

Fullback
Jeffries

Halfback   Halfback
Mullane   Winters (Captain)

Quarterback
Hopkins

End	Tackle	Guard	Center	Guard	Tackle	End
Douglass	Badger	Hemming	Griffin	McGuffey	Jackman	Jones

MARSHALL

End	Tackle	Guard	Center	Guard	Tackle	End
Smith	Everett	O'Toole	Needham (Capt.)	Willets	Bennett	Haldy

Quarterback
Lighthart

Halfback   Halfback
Collins   Trowbridge

Fullback
Budge

Of course, as the sides faced each other the left end of
Chester, Jones, found himself confronting the right end
of Marshall, Haldy. And while the fullback bore the
ominous name of Budge, it was apparent from his
bulky frame that this was just about the last thing he
might be expected to do, for he looked as though a
mountain would not move him.

Silence fell upon the vast throng. If anyone had
ventured to speak above a whisper just at that critical
moment, he would have found himself frowned upon
by a dozen angry persons close by.

Out there in the arena the twenty-two contestants
crouched in their favorite attitudes, and with nerves

strained to the utmost, waited for the ball to be put in action. It was a picture never to be forgotten, and no wonder the eyes of the gathered multitude of spectators remained glued upon the motionless figures, looking like statues of famous gladiators in the arena waiting to battle before a Nero, who by the crook of his thumb, either up or down, would seal their fate eventually one way or the other.

Then all at once there was a sudden concerted movement, every one of the players leaping into life; and from that moment on there would be something constantly doing.

CHAPTER XI

THE STRUGGLE ON THE GRIDIRON

When the struggle first began it looked as though the veteran Marshall players meant to smother their lighter opponents by means of the sheer force of their attack. They immediately carried the ball over into Chester's side of the field, and there was danger of a touchdown before the game had been in progress five minutes.

During this period the Chester spectators sat with a numb feeling clutching their hearts, though they tried their best to assume a confidence they could hardly feel. Their boys were really novices at the business, and it was to be expected, they reasoned, trying to bolster up their waning courage, that at first things would hit the Chester line hard. But just wait a bit, until they began to recover their wind, and Jack Winters was given a fair chance to unmask some of his hidden batteries. "He laughs longest who laughs last," was a saying with a good deal of truth behind it; and anyhow the game was very young yet. Besides, Marshall hadn't scored, after all, it seemed.

A burst of applause broke out that seemed to almost shake the ground, such was its vigor. And apparently most of it came from the excited Chester cohorts, though there were some impartial local admirers of the great game who could readily cheer a daring and brilliant play, no matter on which side it occurred.

What had happened was just this: Winters had carried the ball around the Marshall end for a gain of thirty yards, and when he was finally downed it was far over on Marshall ground. The tables had been suddenly turned, and now it was the home team that was forced to act on the defensive.

Another little gallop, on the part of Joel Jackman this time, gave Chester additional gains, with the ball still safe in their possession. As this evidence of the recuperative power of the new Chester machine was discovered, it seemed as though the vast crowd would go crazy with delight. Even the local rooters grinned their happiness.

"Well! well! well! they *can* do something worth while!" one Marshall student was heard to call out, as though he were indeed surprised. "Why, bless my soul, we're going to see a real game after all, and not a walkaway."

"You needn't worry," snapped a Chester boy close by, full of ginger, and ready to stand up for his colors all the time; "we've got a pretty nest of tricks ready to unload on your fellows. Just keep your eye on Chester, Green, and don't worry. Plenty of time for that after the game is finished, and you hear the real Chester yell!"

Next Fred Badger, given the signal, seized upon the ball when it was snapped to him, and actually smashed his way through left tackle for another gain of twelve yards. His action had evidently taken the Marshall fellows off guard, for they must have anticipated a renewal of the drive around the ends.

Now they were well over on enemy territory, and for the first time in the game a cry began to arise for a touchdown, that only students hungry for a touchdown can emit. Louder and more insistent it grew in volume as the players began to settle back again for a renewal of the desperate tussle. Even many Marshall fellows took part in the demand, for, as they loudly proclaimed, it would make the game much more interesting if their team had a handicap in the start to fight against, since they always did their best work when forced to exert themselves, and come up from behind.

Well, if they were really sincere about it they had their wish speedily gratified. Hardly were the players in motion again than a single figure was seen streaking in like wildfire past the struggling mass, and heading deeper into Marshall territory as though determined that this time nothing should prevent a score.

It was Mullane, the left halfback! As a rule, Steve could hardly be called a genuine sprinter, and doubtless that was just why Jack had selected him for this special occasion, for the lighter fellows would of course be under suspicion, and interference focussed on their actions.

There was pursuit, of course, and it could be seen that Bennett and Haldy were rapidly overtaking the fugitive. Such a wild howl as went up all over the field at this thrilling stage of the game! Mullane dared not look back over his shoulder. By mere instinct alone he understood just what was happening, and how from several quarters Marshall players were closing in on him.

Perhaps he fancied he could even hear their panting just behind him. It must have nerved Steve as nothing else could have done. He knew that he was on the verge of immortal fame, even though he might not secure the coveted touchdown that the mob was now shouting for so hungrily.

It is just such a situation as this that makes a fellow bring to the front hitherto unsuspected energies. Steve certainly never in all his life ran like he did on that particular occasion. Why, some of the delighted Chester boys boasted that he fairly *flew*, as though he had wings suddenly developed; though of course those light-footed pursuers came even faster.

Then, just when Bennett hurled himself to drag Steve down, by a mighty effort the Chester boy threw his body forward, and fell on his face, with the ball gripped fiercely in his hands *over the line!*

When this wonderful fact became evident to the crowd, as it did like magic, the air was rent with mad cheers. Everybody jumped up to wave their hands, school colors, and handkerchiefs; while amidst the terrific din a hundred hats soared heavenward, to be reckoned with afterwards by their reckless and excited owners.

It was a clean touch down for Chester! First blood had after all come to the visitors. The Marshall players began to look more serious. After all, then, it was not destined to be such a "soft snap" as some of them had made out to believe. They had better gird themselves, and start in to do something on their own account. These Chester fellows could play the game, it seemed, for all there was in it. Visions of possible defeat spurred the locals on to increasing their pressure. They remembered that Jack Winters led those hosts from the rival town; and in the baseball session he had demonstrated what a menace he could be to any opponent. Besides, it must not be forgotten that Chester had had the advice and coaching of a veteran college player, who had kept his finger on the pulse of the football world, even though he had been actually out of the real struggle for years.

The kick for goal after the touchdown proved futile. Either the distance was too great, or else a slant of the wind caused the ball to miss its mark, much to the regret of McGuffey, who had qualified for that honor. Jack determined that if another like opportunity occurred he would depend on sturdy Big Bob Jeffries. Now that the thing was done, he realized that this was his first mistake thus far.

But the score was five to nothing, and the fight still on Marshall's lines. It might be possible to duplicate the performance, and still further push the home players down in the mud.

Marshall, however, was now nettled. The sting of that easy touchdown was like the goad to a lazy horse. The whole line quickened, and during the remainder of the first period they forced the fighting over into Chester territory. Indeed, after a number of downs, and a close call from having a touchdown scored upon them, Chester only barely managed to hold the hungry enemy at bay until the referee's whistle announced that the first period had expired.

During the few minutes between the end of the first quarter and the renewal of activities, there was much buzzing of tongues all over the grandstand. Everybody seemed to be talking at once; and of course the three girl chums from Chester had to have their brief say.

"Wasn't it a grand sight, though, to see Steve Mullane carrying the pigskin oval across the line?" exclaimed Lucy Marsh, her eyes snapping in her delight. "Girls, after all, I've decided that I'll attend that barn dance Thanksgiving night out at the Badgeley Farm with Steve. You see, four fellows have asked me, and I hardly knew which one I wanted to accept; but after what Steve has done to cheer up Chester this day, of course I couldn't decline his invitation."

"But please don't say that Steve did it all!" spoke up Mollie Skinner, quickly. "He was only one in the chain, remember, though deserving of great praise for beating those fast runners, and falling across the line with the ball just in time. I noticed that Fred Badger made a distinct gain, without which Steve never could have reaped his reward. Some are given to plant, others to water, but the fortunate one is able to reap the harvest of cheers. It's hardly fair; Fred, yes, and Joel Jackman, too, deserves a share in the applause, for they made that touchdown possible."

"There's glory enough for all," said Adelaide, wisely, to settle the question in a common-sense way. "Every fellow on the team, from Jack Winters down, had a share in that play; for you must have noticed that they interfered and shut off much of the pursuit so that the nearest Marshall boys could not hold Steve when he started his plunge."

"Well, there they are at it again, girls, and what a dandy kick-off that was! Oh! I hope Chester still holds the advantage when this period ends."

Lucy's devout wish seemed without avail, for the fighting soon surged over on Chester territory, with the heavy Marshall machine pushing its way remorselessly forward yard by yard. Before six minutes had passed they had scored a safety from their opponents, giving them two points to start with. Then came a furious struggle ending in a goal being kicked from field that netted Marshall just three points; and as the period finally came to an end they were threatening a repetition of this same system of tactics.

During the intermission Marshall made two changes in their line-up, it being discovered that there were weak links in their chain. Chester had thus far fortunately escaped any serious accidents, and Jack did not give any of the eager substitutes a chance to show what they had in them, though they were ready to jump in at a word.

Jack now saw it was true concerning the ability of several Marshall players to kick amazing field goals, and he realized that it must be his policy after this to try to keep the situation from developing along those lines, and debar them from such opportunities as much as possible.

With the starting of hostilities again the play began to center around midfield. Now it was Chester in possession of the ball, and then like magic it passed into the hands of the locals. Half-way through the quarter the tide surged back on to Chester territory, with all that brawn thrown upon them. Speedily came a touchdown for Marshall, but the kick for goal missed connections by a foot.

When but two minutes remained for a recovery there

came a series of brilliant forward passes on the part of Chester, followed by steady gains, until just as the last minute was starting, Jack gave the signal that brought about a brilliant play, following which Jones, the left end, ran swiftly around and planted the ball across the line for another touchdown. A kick for goal failed to score, and as the whistle of the referee announced that the quarter had come to an end, a mighty howl arose from thousands of throats, while the whole grandstand and field seemed to fairly blaze with innumerable waving flags and pennants and all manner of such objects. For with the game three-quarters finished the score was actually a tie, being ten to ten!

CHAPTER XII

GLORY ENOUGH FOR ALL

The stage was now set for the deciding quarter of the game. Many already began to talk of the result being a tie that would necessitate another test of skill and endurance. Marshall admirers, however, scoffed at such a thing. They tried to make out that thus far their veteran team had only been trifling with the fellows from the rival town. Now that it had reached this stage they were bound to show their real form, and snow poor Chester under.

But somehow this line of talk failed to frighten those who wore the colors of the visiting team. What they had seen convinced them that their faith was in good hands. Jack Winters had yet to go down to defeat since he took charge of outdoor sports in Chester, barring that one fight with Harmony in baseball. No doubt he had managed to inspire his players with some of his own indomitable energy and never-give-up spirit.

So play was resumed where it had been left off, and almost immediately the rival teams were at work, "hammer and tongs," as one gentleman described it. Brilliant plays followed in rapid succession, each accompanied by a burst of applause, which was, however, instantly stilled, as though the crowd understood instinctively how it was necessary that they remain hushed in order that the leaders' signals, and the whistle of the referee, so frequently sounding, might be plainly heard by those who fought in the arena.

After a successful plunge Marshall lost the ball on downs. A punting duel followed, with the advantage slightly in favor of Marshall, though both Mullane and Jeffries managed to hold up their end with considerable honor.

Then came a furious attack on the part of the locals that carried Chester well off its feet. Before they could rally to ward off the blow, a touchdown resulted, though again the kick for goal failed, owing to the flukey wind, as some of the chagrined Marshall players hastened to explain.

It began to look serious for the visitors, with Marshall again in the lead. Time was a factor to be counted on now in deciding matters. All Marshall had to do was to hold their opponents, and they would win. Of course the desire to add to their score would always tempt them to strive further; and this might give Chester the opening needed.

Jack sent the word around for a supreme effort. He felt that they were capable again of turning the tables on the enemy, despite the fact of their superior heft and experience.

When Fred, Joel, and the balance of the boys got that signal they realized how it was now up to them to play like demons. They had apparently been doing the best that was in them hitherto; but strange to say there always seems to be just a little more vim and snap in a football player's make-up that can be summoned to the fore when a desperate situation arises.

All those devoted admirers who had traveled across to Marshall to see them do the old town credit must not be disappointed, if it lay in human endurance to wrest victory from impending defeat.

So spurred on by this incentive, and with their opponents resting under the belief that they had the game already "sewed up," by reason of that last touchdown, Jack's warriors exerted additional pressure, and bent the line back until they were fighting on Marshall territory, grimly pressing on a few yards at a time without a single fumble.

It was thrilling to see how like inexorable Fate they continued to push forward, despite the frantic efforts of the locals to head them off. Again was the crowd on its feet, every eye fastened on the struggling mass of players. Hearts beat high with renewed hope among those Chester onlookers. They realized that this was to be the crowning episode in all the long and bitter contest, when Jack Winters would bring every particle of skill and endurance he could command in his fighting eleven to tear off a victory before the time had expired.

How desperately Captain Needham rallied his players to the defense! It seemed as though they stood like a stone-wall against the rashes of the visitors; and yet in spite of everything Chester managed to continue gaining.

Now it was by a clever swing around the end; again it was a mass play that tore through the center, and took the ball well along for perhaps five or six yards before the runaway was downed. Chester still had the ball, and that was the encouraging feature of it all; Chester meant to hang on to the ball like grim death until the golden opportunity came to try for a touchdown that would once again even up the score, now in Marshall's favor by five points.

There was no talking going on now in the grandstand. Everyone was too much worked up for such a thing. Besides, what with the outbursts of spasmodic cheering, instantly quenched, and the necessity for silence between times, no opportunity for exchanging opinions offered.

Many had their watches out and were casting apprehensive glances at the dials. There remained much less than two minutes of time. Then the referee's whistle must sound to indicate that the game was finally over. Could Chester redeem that loss of a touchdown against such strenuous opposition as those Marshall fellows were now putting up?

Even the most sanguine began to feel doubts gripping their faithful hearts. The boys were doing well, much better than anyone had ever believed possible; but, of course, the gruelling pace must be beginning to tell upon them. They were not seasoned veterans like most of the Marshall fellows; and in such a long and bitterly fought battle on the gridiron experience counts in the last round.

And yet they were still pushing ahead. It was wonderful, grand! How the sight did thrill some of those who years back may themselves have taken part in similar struggles, when in college, or attending a high school; and what vivid memories it must have called to mind as they stood there, holding their very breath, and drinking in the ever changing picture!

If anything was going to be done, there was certainly no more time to lose, for really but a part of a minute still remained. It looked as though, despite their gallant fight, the boys from Chester were doomed to be held back from the victory, or the tie, that was so near.

Then something happened.

A gasp seemed to pass over the throng. Scurrying figures on the field announced that the expected was being carried out. Chester was making a last desperate effort for a touchdown. It would be the expiring flicker of the flame; for whether successful or not it must mark the end, since the referee would be blowing his whistle before play could be resumed.

They saw a figure shoot out ahead of all the rest. Why, what was this - could it be Winters, the halfback, who had the ball, when many had distinctly seen it just a second before in the possession of Fred Badger? The pass had been so cleverly executed that not only had the spectators almost to a man been deceived, but the Marshall players themselves were confused, and in this way last much of their effectiveness.

Fast upon the heels of the flying halfback two Marshall players came dashing; but they might as well have hoped to catch the wind in a sixty-mile gale as overtake that speedy runner. It was as though Jack had reserved his best powers for this special occasion. He saw just where he meant to hurl himself over the line, and clutch that envied touchdown. Had a dozen followed he would have distanced them every one, such was his mettle just then. He seemed endowed with supernatural speed, many who stared and held their breath believed.

Then a roar went up that dwarfed all that had gone before. Jack was over, and had thrown himself, still grasping the ball, for the touchdown that tied the score!

Hardly had this happened when the shrill whistle of the referee announced that the fourth and concluding quarter had ended.

"A tie! a tie!" shrilled hundreds of excited voices.

"Hold on there, you're away off!" others called out, making frantic gestures as they shouted these words. "Don't you see the umpire using his megaphone, and that referee, head linesman, and field judge are waving their arms? Keep quiet, everybody! They've got a communication to make. Perhaps the game isn't *quite* over yet!"

By degrees the uproar quieted down, when it was generally discovered that the umpire had an important communication to make. Evidently the players under-stood just what its nature was going to be, for while the Chester boys looked eager and expectant, those on the Marshall side bore an air of despondency.

"According to the rules of the game, as set down in the official guide," shouted the umpire through his megaphone, so that everybody was able to hear all he had to say, "when a touchdown is made just as play closes for the fourth period an extension of time is to be granted the side making the same, to try for a kick for goal. So Chester is now at liberty to make that try. If it fails, the score remains a tie; if successful, of course the game goes to Chester. Please everybody remain quiet until the test has been made."

This time Jack made no mistake. He beckoned to Big Bob Jeffries to try for goal. It was an oblique slant, and only a clever kicker could succeed, with that baffling wind against him. Big Bob looked once in the direction of the grandstand as if to draw inspiration. Most people believed he must know some girl, whose encouragement he sought; but Mollie and Lucy and Adelaide did not venture to take such honor to themselves. A little modest woman sat behind them, and it was her eyes moist with tears of pride that inspired Big Bob Jeffries when he strode up to win, or know the reason why - his mother sat there!

Well, when the "punk" was heard, every eye followed the sailing ball. It seemed to sag to one side, then again took on a true course, as though guided by some invisible hands.

As it was seen to drop squarely over the bar between the posts the crowd broke into frenzied shouts. Chester had won by a single point! That last kick for goal after Jack had saved the day by his touchdown, had done the business; and the happy visitors could go back home feeling they had a reason to be proud of the scrappy eleven that represented their town on the gridiron.

The final score was 16 to 15.

Mark Overton

CHAPTER XIII

WHEN THE RED FIRE BURNED IN CHESTER

It was such a great victory that the boys of Chester laid plans to celebrate by making a night of it, just as they always do in college towns, when the local team brings home high honors, to be handed down to posterity as great feats worthy of emulation.

On the way back home every fellow in the big carryall promised to come out and join the parade that must circle through every street in town. It would be led by a brass band, and they would march to the glare of numerous bonfires, which of course the younger element could be depended on to furnish. They had already doubtless taken note of every old vegetable barrel that grocers unwittingly left outdoors nights, as well as a few tar barrels in addition, all of which would help make the heavens turn red under the glare, and add to the joyous occasion.

Jack tried to back out, but his mates would accept no excuses.

"You're no more tired than the rest of the bunch, Jack," Toby told him; "and say, what is a victorious procession going to be like, anyway, with the noblest Roman of them all absent? You are the captain of the football squad, and everybody'll expect you to be in the front rank. Just forget all your modesty for once, Jack, and make up your mind to have a grand blowout."

"We certainly deserve it," snapped Joel Jack-man, "after putting up such a royal fight against desperate odds. Why, when it drew near the end I warrant you even the most loyal among our rooters began to turn cold with fear that Chester would be left out in the count. But didn't Packy McGraw and his crowd sing loud, though? That's what a cheer captain can do for his side. Every time I heard them give that Chester yell it seemed to put fresh heart in me."

"'Course you've just got to come out, Jack," protested Steve. "Why, we'll gather around your shack and keep on yelling bloody murder if you refuse, until your folks will show you the door. We want you, and we've got to have you."

So, to "keep peace in the family," as Jack laughingly explained, he consented, although with a shade of doubt.

"Keep things within reason, fellows," he urged them. "Don't let's be too crazy with our success. It's true that we've done our town credit today, and made old Joe Hooker happier than he's been for years, because he believed in us to the end; but let's hold ourselves in some."

"It only happens once a year, as a rule, Jack," said Toby Hopkins, exultantly; "and my stars! we've just *got* to blow off steam after that great time, or bust, that's all."

Later on, after night had fully set in, the racket commenced. Small boys began to set off firecrackers and Fourth of July pistols loaded with blanks. Here and there the first bonfires started, until one could hardly look up and down any street in Chester without discovering one or more burning, with a host of busy little stokers clustering around, and adding fresh fuel to the flames as new stores were brought in by industrious scouts and raiders. It was a wise citizen who, having an ash barrel setting in his yard, had had the forethought to remove it to a place of safety; for the chances were decidedly against its being found in its accustomed spot when dawn came along.

Jack met Big Bob while on his way to the appointed rendezvous of the football boys, where smiling Joe Hooker had also agreed to join them for the parade. Indeed, he had a suspicion that Bob had come out of his way in the hope of finding him at home. This was proven by the first words the other spoke.

"Well, this is luck, Jack," said Bob, as he saw, by the light of a street lamp, whom he had run across. "I was on my way around to make sure you'd come out and join the boys. Then, again, I just wanted to have a few words with you about - you know what I mean, Jack."

"Has anything happened, Bob?" asked the other, quickly.

"If you mean has the mystery been cleared up, I'm sorry to tell you no," Big Bob replied. "But there has been a great change in my home affairs, Jack. It's really wonderful, to me anyhow, because all my life it seems that my father has held me at arms' lengths. Why, Jack, what do you think, when I got home tonight, dirty as anything, and with this bruise on my cheek where I struck the ground that time we had the big smash, would you believe it, he actually shook my hand with a vim, and told me he was proud of me. Why, I tell you that was worth all I did in my humble capacity, to help win the victory, yes, a dozen times over."

Jack did not laugh, although it seemed very humorous to hear a boy make such a strange statement as that. Why, most fathers would have said that much and ten times over; indeed, few could ever have allowed such a gap of coldness to arise between themselves and their own children. It was high time Mr. Jeffries awoke to a realization of the fact that he had a boy of whom any father might well be proud. Yes, he had shirked his duty as a parent long enough; and Jack was glad to know the scales were being lifted from his eyes.

To himself Jack was saying that already it seemed as though great good was coming out of Big Bob's misfortune. What would a dozen lost letters count in comparison with the knowledge that his father had begun to know him, and that the gulf hitherto existing between them was in a fair way of being definitely bridged?

"It's strange how suddenly your father has become interested in boys' sports, Bob," he went on to tell the other. "I happened to run across Mr. Holliday this morning after I saw you, and he told me something that interested me a good deal."

"About my dad, do you mean, Jack?"

"Yes, about him, Bob. Did you ever know he had

contributed money toward paying off what is still due on the new gymnasium? You know Mr. Holliday is the chairman of the citizens' committee that has the financial end of the undertaking in charge."

"Do you really mean it, Jack? My father give money for such a project as that, when I've heard him say many a time that I was wasting every cent I put in baseball togs and such things; and that when he was a boy they had only a pair of skates, or a home-made sled, to have sport with. Tell me more, Jack, please; you've got me all in a flutter now."

"Oh! Mr. Holliday, Adelaide's father, you know, simply said that Mr. Jeffries had awakened at last to a realization of how much athletic sports mean for the health of all boys who love to play ball, and skate, and exercise in a gymnasium, for he had come into his office of his own accord, planked down one hundred dollars in a check, and told the chairman that if when they were making up their tally the funds fell shy to call upon him for another like amount!"

Big Bob gasped, such, was his surprise and delight. He fairly bubbled over when grasping Jack's hand and squeezing it unmercifully.

"Thank you for telling me that, Jack!" he cried. "It's certainly the best thing I've heard this many a long day. I thought I was happy over having had a share in our victory today; but say, that doesn't cut a figure with the way I am thrilled by such glorious news. It means a whole lot to me, Jack. After this I'll have a chance to know my father, and he to understand me better. Oh! if only that one dark cloud could be settled, how happy I'd be! Did that letter go across to England, or was it lost out of my pocket on that fatal occasion when I forgot?"

Jack, knowing that he could not say anything more to comfort Big Bob, tried to relieve the tension by drawing the other's attention to something else.

"We must devote ourselves from now on, Bob, to perfecting a new line of attack," he went on to say. "Every member of the Harmony squad was there in the front row, and simply devouring our methods of assault. Depend on it, they will expect to profit from what they saw today."

"That's a sort of unfair advantage, it strikes me, Jack, since we on our part know so little about their style of play. None of us has seen them practice this season; and I heard that they had completely altered their mode of attack and defense since last year."

"All right, we're going to be given a chance to learn something between now and our Thanksgiving game; because, Bob, as you must know, Harmony and Marshall are due for a fight next Saturday, the one before the day we get busy again."

Bob gave a pleased cry.

"Why, of course, how silly of me to forget that important fact, Jack! And, to be sure, the whole Chester football squad will be bunched close to the line, watching every play that is made, and remembering it for future reference. Do you think they will down poor old Marshall easier than we did?"

"They ought to," came the reply, "because they have a

team that works like a well-oiled machine, I've been told. But wait and see. Lots of sure things in football dope fail to work out when the trial comes off. I've known a team that ran ten pounds heavier all through to be smartly beaten by a more lively bunch, that knew just how to carry the giants off their feet, and keep them from using their great strength. But here we are at the church, and most of the boys seem to be on hand."

It had, of course, been agreed that none of the boys should discard their football togs, though given the liberty of washing up, and making themselves a little more respectable. What would a lot of victors on the gridiron look like in a procession, passing shouting crowds of enthusiastic admirers, if they appeared dressed as if on a Sunday parade?

Old Joe Hooker was also present, bubbling over with joy over the success his proteges had won that afternoon. He freely predicted another strong fight, with a possible victory in sight, when they faced the Tigers of Harmony on Thanksgiving morning.

In due time the procession started. Crowds were in all the main streets, and windows in adjacent houses had been illuminated in honor of the occasion. Chester assumed a really festive air, and what with the mad cheering, and the loud laughter, it soon became evident that there was to be little sleep for anyone until the boys had exhausted themselves, and the supply of barrels, as well as fire-crackers, gave out.

Despite his objections they hoisted Jack on the shoulders of Steve Mullane and Big Bob Jeffries, to lead the van. Then, as though it were only fitting that good old Joe Hooker should share in the occasion, he too was taken in hand, and carried in a chair close to Jack. Amidst whooping crowds they passed, so that everybody might have a chance to set eyes on the pair whom Chester honored that night; while the explosions continued and the red fire burned in the streets.

But it was fated that the glorious day was not to be complete without a touch of tragedy, for along about nine o'clock, when the rioters were beginning to feel too tired to continue the march much longer, and people were returning to their homes in great numbers, a sudden sound rang out that sent a thrill through many hearts.

This was the loud, harsh clang of the fire-bell, telling that a real conflagration was about to add its quota to the excitement of the afternoon and evening.

CHAPTER XIV

WHAT FOLLOWED THE CELEBRATION

"Hey! boys, listen to that, will you? Has the fire-engine company started to join in the celebration?" whooped Phil Parker, who was along with the rest, though barred from the football squad because of an injury to his leg, and also positive orders from headquarters at home to avoid all strenuous sports for some months.

"Not much they haven't, Phil!" cried Joel Jackman, showing signs of growing excitement. "Nothing make-believe about that alarm, let me tell you. There's a genuine fire broken out somewhere around town!"

"Just as like as not some of those reckless kids with their bonfires have gone and done it!" ventured Steve Mullane, indignantly; "and now the people will begin to say how foolish it was to give up the town to this wild orgy of celebration, just because the boys of Chester won a game."

"Listen, will you?" exclaimed still another of the bunch, as they stood there with strained ears, and at the same time casting apprehensive glances around, as though each individual fellow had a haunting dread lest it might turn out to be his own comfortable home that was threatened with destruction.

"Going to be some fire, let me tell you," snapped Fred Badger, "with the wind blowing as strong as it does."

"There, look over yonder, boys, just beyond the spire of the Presbyterian Church! Don't you think it's showing brighter in that quarter? Yes, sir, the fire lies over that way, as sure as anything!"

"Let's gallop along, then," suggested Toby Hopkins impulsively. "No telling when the volunteer firemen will get there, they seem so slow about gathering, and running their old machine to a blaze. Thank goodness! we've decided to have an up-to-date fire department in little old Chester right away. Our town has waked up from her long sleep, and is beginning to stretch and yawn."

They were already in motion before Toby reached the end of his speech, running in pretty much of a bunch; just as though it might be a game of hare-and-hounds that was being started, and the signal had been given to take up the pursuit.

As they dashed along at quite a good speed, the boys could hear cries of interest on all sides. People who had retired to their homes, under the belief that the exciting night's doings were about over, now stood in open doorways. Questions were flung at the boys as they rushed by, the burden of these anxious inquiries being as to the location of the fire.

Of course, as they themselves were still densely ignorant concerning this, none of the bunch could give any coherent answer; though one might fling over his shoulder some reassuring words such as:

"Don't know exactly; but it doesn't seem to be in the mill section!"

Doubtless that brought a sense of relief, for whenever there sprang up a fire in Chester the first fear of everybody was that it might be among the fine structures clustered closely together, and consisting of various busy mills and workshops employing hundreds of persons.

It was a fit night for a big fire, others thought, as they noted how the November wind scurried along with a keen tang, as though the first fall of snow might yet surprise the unsuspecting who may not as yet have laid in their usual winter's supply of coal and wood.

That same wind was just bound to contribute to the fire-laddies' troubles, if the conflagration managed to get a fair start, and other buildings chanced to be close to the one that was burning.

Chester was rather spread out, and covered considerable ground, for it had taken on quite a building boom during the last few years, when new enterprises were started, and more people came to town.

There was no question now but that the boys, hurrying along as they did, were on the right road to the fire. They overtook others bound in the same direction; and as if this were not enough proof to settle the question, they could see that a great light was beginning to flame up, making the sky glow.

"Bet you it's only a grass fire after all!" Jones, the left-end gasped, as he ran lightly along close beside Hemming, the right guard, who had also been a substitute catcher in the baseball days when Steve Mullane held out behind the bat like a stone wall.

"I'd say it was a barn full of hay going up the flue," the other ventured.

No doubt every fellow was hazarding some sort of guess. None of them felt any further personal fear, because they now knew that the blaze was in a section where their homes did not chance to be situated.

"Whee! get that flash of fire, will you?" shouted Big Bob Jeffries, who, despite his heft, managed to keep in the van alongside Jack and Joel and several other fast runners.

All of them had seen it. Through the darkness of the night a tongue of flame had suddenly shot up, and then vanished again; but not before they could notice that dense volumes of smoke hung around the spot.

"What place is it?" called out McGuffey, from the centre of the bunch; "does anybody know?"

"I wouldn't be a bit surprised if it turned out to be that crabbed old miser, Philip Adkins' big house!" ventured Joel; who had often come around this way on his wheel on errands, and ought to be as well acquainted with the locality as anyone, it would seem.

"Right for you, Joel; that's just whose house it is!" echoed another boy, as well as he could utter the words, considering that he was already beginning to get short of breath.

They all knew of Philip Adkins, who had long been

quite a character about Chester. He was said to be quite well-to-do, though those who called him a millionaire were doubtless "drawing the long bow," as people always do whenever the wealth of a miser is under consideration.

Philip Adkins lived in a big house that was unpainted; but those who had had the opportunity of seeing the inside always said he did not stint himself in the way of comfort at all, and that he was only a "peculiar" man. He had one great grudge against the world it seemed. Other boys were straight and healthy, but for some unaccountable reason Heaven had seen fit to give him a crippled grandson. Little Carl Adkins was a pitiable looking object. They sometimes saw him shut up in a closed carriage, and being whisked through the town; but few had ever been able to pass a word with the poor boy. These reported that he was really bright, and had a woe-begone look on his drawn white face, as though his life had known little of joy.

His grandfather hated the sight of other lads, because they reminded him that his boy had none of their abounding health and good looks. He loved the child almost fiercely, partly on account of the boy's misfortune. They said he kept a servant whose main duties were just to attend to little crippled Carl.

Jack remembered an occasion when by sheer accident he had chanced to be passing close to the property of the so-called miser, when he heard a soft "Hello, there!" and glancing up discovered a white, peaked face amidst some vines covering a stone wall. He had heard something about the strange habits of Philip Adkins, and how jealously he guarded his deformed grandson from coming in contact with the outside world, under the belief that people would pity the lad, and some be rude enough to mock his misfortunes.

Jack had stopped and given the little fellow a friendly smile. He had even spoken to Carl, and when the boy eagerly answered him, entered into quite an animated little chat, replying to many feverish questions the other poured out, mostly concerning the things he knew other boys did, for he was a great reader, that being his one enjoyment.

Although their little talk was broken off by the sudden coming of the man-servant who looked after the crippled boy, Jack had never forgotten the last words Carl spoke to him:

"Oh! what wouldn't I give if grandfather would let me just *watch* other boys play ball, and fish, and go in swimming!"

Jack had somehow never told any one of his little encounter with the crippled boy, but those plaintive words often rang in his ears. He had even wondered sometimes whether it would do any good if he should seek an interview with the crabbed, cross-grained old man, and try to persuade him to change his belief that he was doing right in sheltering the cripple from a rude world. But up to the present Jack had not been able to make up his mind to attempt such a bold thing.

And now, what if it turned out that this was the house that was afire, possibly set ablaze through some spark that had been carried by the wind, and lodged where it could communicate to some waste material. A peculiar sense of "coming events casting a shadow before" assailed Jack. He had a vague idea that there might prove to be more about this than mere accident. Sometimes a strange "Destiny shapes our ends," he remembered reading, "rough-hew them as we may." Mr. Adkins had determined that his poor grandson, whom he passionately loved, should be sheltered from stinging criticism, and not allowed to mingle with his kind; but perhaps a power stronger than his will might take affairs in hand, to guide him along a new path, as his eyes were opened to the light.

There was now no longer any doubt concerning the identity of the doomed structure. Joel loudly declared it to be the Adkins house, beyond question.

"And let me tell you, fellows, it's going to be a tough job for our firemen to save any part of the old building, because the blaze has got such a good start I reckon old Philip will have to put up a really modern house in place of the old rookery."

"He's got the cold cash to do it, boodles of the stuff!" panted Phil Parker.

The Adkins house was surrounded with fair-sized grounds, in which no doubt the little prisoner took his daily constitutionals, crutches in hand, though his world must indeed have seemed exceedingly small to the poor chap.

The gate was now open, and people pouring in through the gap, all expressing a great interest in the prospect of any part of the structure being saved.

"But you can depend on it the old fellow has got it well insured," one man was saying to another as they pushed through the opening. "Trust old Philip for always looking out for the safe side. But she'll make a big blaze before they manage to get enough water going to smother the flames."

Just then the boys pushing closer toward the house that stood amidst clouds of billowing smoke saw some one rushing frantically about. It was old Philip Adkins himself, and he certainly looked almost crazed with excitement. At first, as was only natural, the boys rested under the belief that it was the possible loss of his house and its contents that made him act so wildly; but when they heard what he was shrieking they realized that he had good cause for acting so.

"Oh! won't some of you *please* go in and save my poor boy? I believed his attendant was with him, and had carried Carl out; but the man had slipped away after putting his charge to bed, and was over in town, amusing himself in a tavern, I've just found out. Save the poor child, and name your own reward, for I'll go mad if anything happens to my boy!"

CHAPTER XV

IN THE BURNING HOUSE

Something must have happened to delay the coming of the firemen, for as a rule they were prompt to reach the scene. Possibly their engine had broken down again, as had happened once before; which accident caused such a talk that public sentiment was aroused, with the result that a new, modern auto-engine was ordered, and a paid department arranged for.

"Look here, boys, we ought to do something about this!" exclaimed Jack Winters, thrilled with what he had heard the sobbing old man cry out.

Philip Adkins turned toward him frantically. He certainly did not hate boys just at that moment in his life, when it seemed that perhaps he would have to depend on them for the help he was demanding.

"Oh! don't lose any time, I beg of you!" he cried. "I tried to rush indoors myself, but some men caught hold of me, and said I'd surely smother in the smoke. If I thought my poor Carl was lost, nothing could keep me from going in. Save my boy for me, and any favor you ask will be granted; but hurry! hurry, or it will be too late!"

Jack saw that the old man was wild with fear. He reached out and took hold of him by the arm.

"Get a grip on yourself, Mr. Adkins," he said, in that steady voice of his that generally acted so soothingly on those whom Jack addressed. "We'll try to get him out for you. But first tell me where his room is?"

"Upstairs at the first turn; but the hallway is full of smoke by now, and oh! I even fear the fire has reached there!" cried the old man, wringing his hands pitifully as he spoke.

"Try to point out the window of his room to me!" continued Jack, steadily.

Eagerly Mr. Adkins consented to do so, even dragging the boy around with him as he thrust up a hand and with trembling finger pointed upward.

"That one you see with the sash lowered. We try to keep him from any chilly draughts. When you push up the front stairs you must turn to the left, and enter the small passage. Don't lose any more time, or it will be too late! Go! please go!"

"We might make a human chain, and push up the stairs that way," suggested Phil Parker. "Then, even if one fellow does get dizzy inhaling all that terrible smoke he won't be apt to drop down. Jack could be at the end of the chain, always pushing ahead as we added on to it here at the open door!"

Some of the others seemed to think that a pretty clever idea, judging from the exclamations that arose all around. But Jack believed he knew what might be a safer way than the scheme thus proposed.

"Hold on," he told the others, "I've got an idea that beats yours all hollow, Phil. Leave it to me, fellows."

With that Jack sprang forward.

"I understand what he's got in his head!" cried Toby Hopkins. "It's the grape-arbor! Don't you see it lies just under that window. Fact is, a fellow can climb right up to the sash as easy as anything."

"Bully boy, Jack; you know how to manage it all right!" exclaimed Steve, admiringly, though truth to tell he had never once doubted but that Jack would discover a means to the end, as he nearly always did.

Jack was climbing fast. He knew that in a case like this seconds count. That pungent wood smoke was a terrible thing, and if Carl lay helpless at its mercy for a given period of time the chances were no power on earth could restore the little cripple to life; for his constitution was far from robust at the best, and consequently he must succumb much more speedily than would a stronger boy.

Beaching the top of the arbor Jack started to crawl along the bars heading toward the window. He had already arranged his simple plan of campaign. There was indeed only one thing he could do, which was to enter the room, and finding the lad manage in some fashion to get him to the window, and down to the ground.

"Be ready down there when I want your help!" he shouted to the rest of the gang; for what with the loud cries of new arrivals and the crackling of the flames close by it was necessary to raise one's voice in order to be heard.

One look downward Jack took just before he arrived at the side of the house. It was light enough now to see easily, for the fire had broken through, and the entire grounds seemed illuminated with the glow. He saw the faces of his numerous comrades turned upward toward him, intently watching his progress. And others had gathered around, too, intensely interested in the outcome of the affair; for they realized that it was a rescue that the football player had in hand.

There amidst the rest Jack picked out the weazened-up face of the old man. He would never so long as he lived forget that, there was such a world of apprehension, of piteous appeal in the look old Philip Adkins was bending upon him; as though all his remaining hopes of a little happiness in this world centered now upon the gallant boy who had undertaken to save his Carl.

Then Jack reached the side of the house. It felt warm to his touch, a fact that gave him a sudden fear that the worst might have happened to the crippled boy beyond the window.

One effort he made to raise the sash, but it seemed stuck, or else was locked. There was no time for halfway measures, and accordingly Jack, tearing loose a broken section of a wooden bar that formed part of the top of the trellis, smashed the window with several blows, after warning those below to get from under.

He took pains to clear the sash from any projecting

fingers of glass that might have given him trouble in the shape of severe cuts. Then without another glance at the spectators gathered below the boy proceeded to crawl swiftly through the opening, heedless alike of the smoke that was oozing forth in thick volumes, or the possibility of his striking the fire itself, once he had entered the house.

They saw his heels vanish through the gap. Something like a gasp arose from some of the gathered crowd, constantly augmented as fresh arrivals came running up, to ask what had happened, and who it was they saw entering through that window.

Some seemed to consider it a rash thing to do. These for the most part were women who had not yet grasped the fact that Jack was not risking his life out of sheer bravado, but that it was believed the poor little cripple had been abandoned in his room through mistake, and it was Jack's intention to save him if he could.

Then their opinions changed like magic, for their hearts filled with sympathy. Even the sobbing old man became an object of pity, though up to then few in the crowd had been heard to express any sorrow because it was Philip Adkins' house that was afire. This was owing to his unpopularity in Chester, where he never gave to any charitable object, or for that matter even treated folks decently in his bitterness toward all mankind because his poor boy was so deformed, and stricken by a cruel Fate.

The football boys, however, felt none of those fears. They knew Jack Winters' ways, and that he always did what he attempted, if it lay within the range of human possibilities. Although he had gone from their sight they continued to stand there in a bunch, ready to catch the child if Jack dropped him from the window.

One there was who did not seem content to just stand and wait. Joel Jackman was built upon too nervous lines for that; and just as soon as he had seen the last of Jack through the broken window he started up after his leader. Some of the other fellows called to him to come back, but Joel knew what he was about, and gave no heed to their cries.

Jack might need help, he argued with himself, and in that case his arm would come in handy. There was surely enough of them below to do all that was necessary, so that his absence would not count for much. And after all perhaps Joel would prove to be right in his surmise.

Meanwhile Jack had entered the room.

He found it full of pungent smoke that filled his eyes, and made them smart in a way that was almost unbearable. Of course under such conditions he could not distinguish a single thing, and would have to depend on groping his way around.

But it could not be a very large apartment, he figured, and the bed on which little crippled Carl lay must be against the wall. So he immediately started to go the rounds, feeling with his hands in front of him. Foot by foot he went, coming in contact first of all with some sort of dresser that evidently stood between the windows, for there were two in the room, the other having its shutter closed, probably in order to keep out the light to a certain extent.

Still onward Jack pressed, groping as he went. He shut his eyes, for sight was next to useless under such trying conditions, and the smart of the wood smoke almost unbearable.

Then to his satisfaction he stumbled against what proved to be the side of a bed. Eagerly he bent lower, and began to feel among the clothes. He was thrilled when he actually touched something that seemed like a human form, though Jack felt a wave of feeling pass over him when he realized that it was the poor boy's distorted back that he had first of all come in contact with.

Tenderly, eagerly he gathered some of the bedclothes around the figure. There was not the least sign of life or animation about the boy. He might be dead for all Jack could tell; but no matter, he must be saved from those cruel approaching flames.

Having bundled him up the best he could, under such trying conditions, Jack gathered the little chap in his arms. He felt a glow in the region of his heart just then, such as anyone engaged in a mission of rescue might experience. But then, it was only a little thing to do, Jack thought; he really took no risk, and had he held back he would never have forgiven himself for allowing prudence to sap his desire to render assistance.

Now for the window again. He looked around him in vain. His eyes were blinded by the smoke so that he could not tell in which direction he must go in order to come upon the exit.

Baffled in this one respect, that of vision, Jack turned

to another of his senses. He knew there must be a draught setting toward the opening, from which smoke was pouring so heavily. So he set to work endeavoring to learn which way the air moved, knowing that in this fashion he could grope his way to the exit.

Those outside were becoming a bit worried. No doubt seconds had been magnified into minutes in their minds, and they began to have fears that something had happened to the daring lad who had ventured within the building. Every eye remained glued upon the place of his disappearance.

Joel had before then succeeded in reaching the open window, where he crouched and waited, occasionally peering in as if half tempted to crawl through the gap after Jack.

He had hard work contenting himself to remain there on his precarious perch; indeed, only that he did not wish to seem to be interfering with Jack's plans Joel certainly would have ventured across the window sill. Unable to beep silent any longer, he finally gave a loud shout:

"This way out, Jack! Here's the window, over this way!"

CHAPTER XVI

JACK SPEAKS FOR LITTLE CARL

That was a bright idea on the part of Joel, cowering there at the window, and dodging the dense volume of smoke that poured forth as through a funnel. For Jack heard the call, and it gave him a clue as to where the window lay. So presently he arrived there, greatly to Joel's delight.

"Oh! you've got the poor little chap then, have you, Jack? Is he dead or alive?" was what he burst out with, as he became aware of his friend's presence.

"I don't know," Jack replied; "but we must get him down as quick as we can, Joel, so a doctor can work over him. He may not be too far gone yet from the smoke. The fire never touched him. Do you think we could manage it between us, by taking all manner of care?"

"Sure thing, Jack. Here, let me hold him some while you climb out. Hang that awful smoke, it makes the tears blind you!"

A shout arose from the anxious crowd below. Jack did not dare waste even seconds in glancing down, but he could imagine the old man stretching his hands up mutely as though imploring the rescuers to hasten, so as to relieve the tension of his breaking heart.

Cautiously they began to make their way along over the top of the trellis. Jack only feared lest some strip of rotten wood might give way under their combined weight, and allow them to plunge downward. A solid phalanx of the sturdy football players had formed directly beneath, and they seemed determined that if anything of this sort took place they would serve as a buffer, so that those who fell through might not be seriously injured.

But no accident befell them, and soon they were being assisted down the arbor by willing hands. The old man fought his way into the midst, nor did anyone have the heart to deny him this privilege, understanding how frantic he must be to learn the worst.

A gentleman pushed forward.

"Here's Doc. Halleck!" cried Phil Parker, just then recognizing one of the town physicians, who with the rest had hurried to the spot, possibly being at the time on his night round of visits to patients, and thinking that perhaps the services of a doctor might be needed at the fire.

He took the bundled form of the cripple from Jack. Old Mr. Adkins hung over the boy as though everything he had in the wide world could go up in flames if only he might be told that the child was all right. In that minute of time people who had looked down on the old miser with scorn began to realize that he was capable of human affection, and that he actually had a heart.

Carrying the lad to some little distance from the house, to be out of the way of the firemen when they arrived and set to work with their apparatus, Doctor Halleck laid his burden on the ground. Then he called for some water, and the old man told one of the boys how to get a supply from the well close by.

When this was fetched, the physician, who had already been holding a small phial containing ammonia, Jack suspected, to the cripple's nose, set to work to bathe his patient's face with the cool liquid.

"Oh! tell me the worst, Doctor, please!" begged old Mr. Adkins, wringing his hands as, by the light of the fire, he looked at the white face of little Carl, seemingly so corpse-like. "Is he dead, my poor, poor boy?"

"Nonsense, Mr. Adkins, he will be all right inside of five minutes," said the doctor, brusquely, for like many other people he had never liked the old miser. "He has inhaled considerable of the smoke, and must have fainted away up there in his room, after calling out for help without being heard. I give you my word, sir, there is nothing serious the matter with him; though had he remained in that terrible atmosphere a short time longer all efforts to resuscitate him would be in vain. You owe a lot to the boy who brought him out in time, let me tell you, sir."

At that the old man turned upon Jack Winter, and clutched his hand almost fiercely. He was about to pour out a torrent of words telling how grateful he felt, when to the great relief of the boy a shout arose that drowned everything else out.

"Here comes the engine at last! Now watch the boys get busy!"

A roar went up as the red-shirted firemen with their helmets and their waterproof garments came rushing into the grounds. A babel of confusion followed, as they demanded to know where they could get connection with the nearest fire hydrant on the street, or if none were handy where could the cistern be found!

Jack broke away and went with the rest of the boys to lend a hand if anything could be done to assist the fire-fighters. It was learned that a hydrant stood handy not a hundred feet distant, and to this a hose was attached without delay. Meanwhile the engine was run alongside a cistern, and set to work, the loud pumping soon telling that operations had been started.

When the first stream of water was seen pouring into an open window a cheer arose from the crowd. Of course few expected that there would be much left of the building but the bare walls, for the fire had by this time gotten a good start, and was being whipped by the night wind; but then they did not bother to waste any sympathy upon the owner, after once learning who he was.

It was a spectacular and fitting climax to the night's celebration, just as though Nature wished to add her mite to the glorification on account of the victory Chester's boys had won on the gridiron that day.

For some time it was a fight between the rival elements, fire against water; and as the former had obtained a good start it proved to be a difficult thing to head it off. Here, there and in many places the flames would break forth, and eat up whole sections of the frame building, despite the vigorous efforts of the firemen to control them. Fortunately there was no house near enough to be caught in the whirlwind of flames that poured furiously forth from time to time. A myriad of red sparks flew on the wind; but those who lived in the quarter whence they went were doubtless taking all necessary precautions to prevent damage, even to wetting the roofs of their dwellings with the garden hose, or by means of buckets.

Taken in all, it was a pretty lively time in Chester, and one not soon to be forgotten either. The fire burned well through the house. It would have gone like a bundle of shingles only that the flames had started at the leeward end, and consequently had to eat their way against the wind.

Some of the boys had gone home, well tired out, but a number of them still hung around, and seemed bent on staying as long as Jack Winters did. If he had seen old Mr. Adkins approaching, Jack might have tried to slip away, but he was unaware of the fact, though Joel and Toby knew it, and exchanged nods, while refraining from putting the other on his guard.

So suddenly Jack found himself once more seized upon by Philip Adkins. The miser was looking a thousand per cent better than before. That agonized expression had left his face, and something seen there caused Toby to say aside to Joel, "He almost looks human."

"You are the boy who saved my Carl's life!" exclaimed Mr. Adkins, in a voice that trembled with emotion, all the while he was clinging to Jack's hand as though he did not mean to let him go free. "They tell me that your name is Jack Winters, and that you are a comparatively new boy in Chester. I don't remember hearing of you before, but they say you have taken the lead of the boys here in town, and that everybody is talking about the influence you have with them. You have done me a great favor this night, Jack Winters. That poor little fellow, tortured as he is by a cruel Nature, is dearer to me than most boys are to their parents. I told you to ask me any favor you could think of, and if it was within my means I'd gladly respond. Even now I'd be glad to know something that I could do, just to prove to everyone how grateful an old man like me can be. Isn't there anything I can do for you, Jack Winters?"

The other fellows listened, and their eyes gave indication of how they considered this the golden opportunity in Jack's life. Why, to have an old miser worth all sorts of money say he would like to bestow anything in his power on a boy, to show his gratitude, was an event that only came to most fellows in dreams.

Jack had a sudden inspiration. It seemed to him that he could again see the pitiful look on the white face of the cripple, and once more hear little Carl saying so sadly:

"Oh! what wouldn't I give if my grandfather would only let me *watch* other boys play ball, and fish, and go in swimming!"

"I'll tell you something you can do, Mr. Adkins, since you seem bent on thinking my little assistance needs compensation; and I'm going to hold you to your promise, sir. In the first place, please alter your opinion of the boys of Chester. They are not the gang of young

Mark Overton

ruffians you've been picturing to yourself, when you set your mind on keeping your grandson from coming in contact with them. They would never taunt him, or make fun of his misfortune, sir, I give you my word for that. They would only feel very sorry that he couldn't have all sorts of fun like they enjoyed; and if it lay in their power at any time I assure you every fellow would go far out of his way to give little Carl a good time.

"I hope I'm not overbold in saying this to you, Mr. Adkins; but one day I happened to have a little chat with Carl, who hailed me from the top of the wall where he had climbed. And, sir, if you could have heard the longing in his voice when he said to me at parting: 'Oh! what wouldn't I give if my grandfather would only let me *watch* other boys play ball, and fish, and go in swimming!' Don't you see you are starving his soul by keeping him away from everybody? Some day, if he lives, he must face the world, and you're keeping him from getting used to it now. Please think this over, Mr. Adkins, and let him mingle with boys of his age. You'll never regret it, I'm sure, and it would be the best thing for the boy that could happen. You'll soon see color come in his face, and his eyes will take on a different look from the one of pain and dread they have now. And the first boy who offends that little cripple will have to reckon with me, sir, I give you my word for it!"

"And with me, too," snapped Fred Badger, trying hard to keep from letting his eyes betray the fact that he was near crying; for Jack's earnest plea, and the thought of the lonely life the little cripple had been leading greatly affected Fred.

Other boys added their assurances to what had already been said. Mr. Adkins was plainly much impressed. He showed it by the way he stared around at the circle by which he was surrounded. Jack held his breath with suspense. He wondered if he had made the impression he hoped for when saying what he did. Strange, how things had worked to bring matters to this focus.

"I *will* think it over, Jack," said the old man, presently. "I already begin to find my eyes opened to the fact that I have sadly misjudged the Chester boys all these years. This almost tragic event may be what was needed to lift the scales from my distorted vision, and enable me to see clearly. Yes, I will think it over, and let you know the result very soon. If I can convince myself that it would be for that dear child's benefit there is nothing from which I would shrink."

And after the boys had seen him depart, once more hurrying back to where Carl lay bundled up in blankets, every fellow insisted on shaking Jack's hand, and telling how his feat in saving the cripple was overshadowed in his victory over the crabbed old boy-hating miser.

CHAPTER XVII

THE AFTERMATH OF A GOOD DEED

"Well, this is the last chance we'll have to practice our secret signal codes before we run foul of Harmony in the big game tomorrow!" said Joel Jackman, on Wednesday afternoon, as he and several other of the team arrived at the same isolated field, where we saw them working under the direction of old Joe Hooker on that previous occasion when Jack and Joel discovered the presence of spies, who later on turned out to be three little maids from school, deeply interested in the doings of the boys, and watching the play through a pair of opera glasses.

"Yes, tomorrow morning is the grand and glorious occasion when we hope to more than duplicate our past performance with Marshall," laughed Fred Badger.

Joel cast a quick glance across the field. Jack smiled when he saw that his attention was centered on the big oak, in the branches of which they had found Mollie Skinner and her two girl chums snugly ensconced.

"Still thinking of that other time, eh, Joel?" he asked, as the other caught his eye and turned a little red.

"Why, you see, it's this way, Jack," stammered Joel; "I

honestly believe those girls were our mascots. They said they meant to wish, and hope, and pray that we'd win the game against Marshall, and sure enough we did that same thing. Now, why shouldn't history repeat itself, I'd like to know? Suppose we did discover 'em peeking again, wouldn't it make you believe we were bound to down Harmony tomorrow? I'm not given much to superstition, but I own up I could see something like a good sign about that sort of thing."

"Well, I happen to know that Mollie, for one, is over at her grandmother's in Springfield today," spoke up Fred Badger, who of course had heard about the visit of the trio of high school girls to the big oak, and how Jack and Joel had to climb up and help them get back to earth again. "But she'll be on hand for the game tomorrow; in fact, she expects to be home tonight."

"Oh! leave it to little Freddy to know all about the movements of Miss Mollie Skinner," crowed Phil Parker somewhat derisively; but then no one paid much attention to what Phil said, because it was well known that the said Fred had cut him out of Mollie's favors, for once upon a time she and Phil had gone together to singing-school and parties.

They found most of the boys assembled, and waiting for the coming of the coach, who had faithfully promised to be on hand that afternoon, in order to go over the various signal codes again. Joe Hooker had not yet put in an appearance, and several of the substitutes were enjoying themselves punting the ball, doubtless also wondering if they were going to be as luckless as before about breaking into the game, this time with Harmony's Tigers.

"Jack," remarked Toby Hopkins just then, "I want to know what's happened to keep you chuckling to yourself right along. I never knew you to do such a thing except when you had something *especially* pleasant to communicate."

"Do you know," spoke up Steve, "I was just thinking the same thing, Toby. More than a few times I've seen Jack look around at the rest of us, and grin as if he felt almost tickled to death over something."

"Well, I am," calmly remarked the object of this attack.

"Then why don't you up and tell the whole bunch what's in the wind, Jack?" asked Joel. "It isn't fair to keep it to yourself hoggishly, is it, fellows?"

"We demand that you confess, Jack!" said Big Bob, sternly.

Jack beckoned to the fellows who were knocking the ball about.

"Come over here, all of you, and gather around me," he said, pretending to look very serious, but not making a great success of it. "I've got something to communicate that may please the bunch, for it concerns every one of us, as well as all other boys in Chester."

"Then it must be about the new gymnasium, Jack!" exclaimed Fred.

"Some one has given the project another boost," ventured Phil Parker. "I wonder now if your dad, Bob, has planked down more hundreds after what he's already donated. Is that it, Jack?"

"Mr. Jeffries has already done his whole duty in the matter, and proven his interest in Chester boys," said Jack. "There happens to be another gentleman in the town who up to date had a pretty poor opinion of boys in general, but who's had a change come over him, a revolutionary change, I should say, because he'd been in to see Mr. Holliday, asking for facts and figures, and then binding himself to stand for every dollar still needed to put the gymnasium on a firm footing, without going one cent in debt!"

The boys held their breath for just five seconds. Then, as if by some concerted signal, they burst out into one great shout, while several threw their extra sweaters high in the air, as though bound to give expression to the state of their feeling in some exuberant fashion.

"Great news this you've brought us today, Jack!" cried Steve Mullane, his honest face lighted up with joy. "Now, what generous gentleman do we have to thank for putting the project on such a solid basis as that? All the boys of Chester will for ages to come feel bound to honor his memory."

"What ails you, Steve, not to be able to guess ?" Toby demanded. "Have you forgotten what happened the night after we licked Marshall, and the Adkins house burned to the ground? Am I right in my guess, Jack, and was this grand present made in the name of little Carl Adkins?"

"You've hit the nail on the head, Toby," admitted the leader of the football squad. "It was old Philip Adkins, and Mr. Holliday said to me that he had never seen such a change as has taken place in that man. Why, he's smiling all the time now, and has been known to stop and watch street boys playing marbles in the vacant lots, or kicking an old fake football around in the side streets of town. Seems like the old gentleman had just waked up, and begun to understand that boys have their appointed place in the whole fabric of animated Nature, as Mr. Holliday expressed it to me in his poetic way."

"Go on and tell us all about it, Jack," urged several, as they continued to press around and listen to all that was being said.

"There isn't such a lot to tell, fellows," protested Jack. "Mr. Adkins told me he would think matters over, and it seems that he has come to a sensible conclusion. He signed an agreement with the chairman of the gym. committee of finances, binding himself to pay all bills outstanding after the present collections have been taken up. I understand that this will be something like six thousand dollars, so you can see that after all it sometimes pays to have a converted miser in any community."

"Just what it does," agreed Steve, "because, once he sees things at their true value, he's apt to give a heap more liberally than some tightwads who never have had to turn over a new leaf."

"So you see," continued Jack, "we'll not have to worry any more as to how the balance of the debt is going to be paid. When we open our new and wonderful gym, containing all sorts of up-to-date appliances for physical development, there will be no debt hanging over our heads. We figured on having to give all sorts of entertainments the coming winter, from basket-ball matches to minstrel performances, in order to raise funds to help out; but now we can devote our time to having all the fun going. You also remember the big promise several of the mill-owners made, led by Mr. Charles Taft?"

"They agreed that if we could work wonders, and get the gymnasium fully paid for when it started, they'd guarantee having a salaried physical instructor engaged who would be there week in and week out, ready to devote his entire attention to the job of building up weak bodies, and giving counsel to those who might strain themselves too much all at once. Yes, and everybody agreed that if any such instructor were engaged we'd all vote to have our dear old Joe Hooker installed. Well, that dream is going to come true also. Joe has signed for a year and will begin his new duties on the first day of December, so that he can be present to see that the apparatus is all properly installed in the gym. when it arrives."

Again a mighty shout attested to the love those fellows felt for smiling Joe, the old-time college player, who had been such a helpful instrument in building up a winning baseball nine, and now a football eleven, in Chester.

"There never was and never will be again a town more highly favored by fortune than little old Chester," affirmed Steve Mullane, when he could make himself heard above all the wild clamor. "While the spirit is strong within us, fellows, let's give three cheers, first for Mr. Philip Adkins, the boys' best friend; and then another series for our own beloved Joe."

"There he comes now, hurrying along, with a limp, and waving his hand to us!" exclaimed another boy.

The cheers were given with a will. Joe waved his hand again in greeting. He must have guessed that they had heard about the contract he signed that same morning in the office of his employer, Mr. Charles Taft, whereby he agreed to be responsible for the upbuilding of the new gymnasium, and the character of its many boy members, for the period of a whole year, devoting his energies to the task, even as his heart was already enlisted in the work.

"Is there anything else you want to tell us before we settle down to business, Jack?" asked Toby Hopkins.

"Just one more thing," replied the other, still smiling. "It concerns that poor little cripple and hunchback, Carl. He has a really wonderful mind, once you get to know him, as so many of his type seem to have; as though Nature to make amends for having cheated them out of so many pleasures connected with boy life had given an additional portion of intellect. Mr. Adkins came over to our house especially to see me last night. Now although he completed those arrangements with the chairman of the financial committee yesterday he never once mentioned the fact to me. What he did say was that he had thought my proposition over carefully, and was convinced that after all he had made a terrible mistake in trying to shield Carl from contact with the world that some day, if he lived, he must mingle with. So he has determined that the boy shall go in and out as he wishes, meet other boys, take the little knocks as others do, and have something to do with the sports boys love so dearly. Of course he won't be able to run, or attempt most things; but he can see others doing them, and that will give him almost as much pleasure. Why, fellows, Mr. Adkins fairly cried when he told me how the poor little chap hugged him after he learned what big revolution was coming about in his daily life. But here's Joe on hand, and ready to put us through our last signal drills; so let's forget everything, except the game with the Harmony Tigers tomorrow morning."

CHAPTER XVIII

BIG BOB BRINGS NEWS

When his mother told Jack he was wanted at the 'phone on Thanksgiving morning shortly after he finished his breakfast, he had a queer little feeling down in the region of his heart, as though something was going to happen.

"I've been half expecting it," he said to himself, as he hurried to the stair landing, where the small table with the receiver stood, handy to those above and below. "It would be pretty tough now if some fellow called me to say he couldn't show up this morning for the game, because he had been taken with the colic during the night, and was as weak as a cat. Hello, there!"

"Jack, are you through breakfast?" asked a voice.

"Oh! it's you, is it, Big Bob?" Jack went on to say, his fears in no way relieved by the discovery of the identity of the one who had called him up. "Yes, I'm through eating. What's up?"

"I'm coming over right away, Jack. Got to see you - very urgent!"

Jack groaned. Then the blow was about to fall, and

Chester would be deprived of their best full-back. No one else could be depended upon like Big Bob for kicking a field goal, or one after a touchdown.

"All right, come along. I'll try to brace myself to stand it!" he said.

Bob did not make any further comment, but just before Jack caught the click as of a receiver being placed on the hook, he thought he heard a sound that was either a chuckle or a grunt, he did not know which.

So he waited for the other to make his appearance, waited, and puzzled his head in the endeavor to guess what Bob would have to say, inventing all sorts of possible excuses for wanting to give up connection with the game. Jack was grimly determined that he would not let go his hold on the big fullback until the last gasp. Surely he must be able to advance some argument that would have weight with any objections the other might raise.

But there was Bob coming as fast as he could walk, even breaking into a little run at times. His case must indeed be a desperate one to make him act like that. Jack went to the door to meet him, thinking the worst. Of course, just at the last hour as it might be Bob's father had put the vital question to him, asking squarely if he could vouch for it that he had mailed that important letter; and poor Bob had to confess his shortcoming. Then Mr. Jeffries, with a return of his old-time sternness, had told the offender that in punishment he should not be allowed to participate in the great Thanksgiving morning game with boasting Harmony.

It was too bad, and Jack felt his heart sink within him like lead. The morning had up to then seemed so crisp and promising that he had been telling himself how even Dame Nature favored the football rivals, and that everything was fine; but now all of a sudden the whole aspect seemed to change.

He had refrained from opening the front door until Bib Bob mounted the steps, on account of the cold wind that would enter. Now as he swung it wide to allow the other passage Jack gave a tremendous start.

"See here, what's this mean? You don't look as if you brought bad news along with you, Big Bob?" he fairly gasped, clutching the other by the arm.

The Jeffries boy was grinning for all he was worth. Jack could not remember ever looking upon a face that seemed so utterly joyous. His eyes were dancing, and there was a flush in his cheeks that did not even confine itself to that portion of his round face, for Big Bob was as red as a turkey-gobbler strutting up and down the barnyard to the admiration of his many wives.

"Bad news, Jack!" exclaimed the other in a half-choked voice; "well, I should say not. It's the most *glorious* news I'm rushing over here with this fine morning. No one could have given me a more delightful surprise than I got just a little while ago. Jack! I *did* mail that letter, of course I did, silly that I was to ever doubt such a thing!"

"How do you know now that you did?" asked Jack, thrilled with satisfaction, while he dragged the other into the hall so that he might close the front door.

"Why, while we were just finishing breakfast who should stop at the house but Mr. Dickerson himself. He said an important letter had arrived for father, and as he was on his way back home to have his breakfast according to his usual habit between mails, he though he'd fetch it along with him; for father and he are very good friends, you must know, and Jack, when I saw that it was from London, you - well, you could have knocked me over with a feather I was so excited. Father read it, and I heard him tell mother that *two* of his letters did get across after all. So you see, Jack, he took a hint from that article we left for him to see, and used the follow-up style of correspondence. I've figured it all out, and know that a steamer carrying a third letter couldn't have had time to get there. Besides, I heard father say it was the first, and also the second letter that landed, for his correspondent told him he had just received a copy of the original, and hastened to reply to both."

Jack seized the other's willing hand, and the two indulged in a mutual squeezing affair, in which the honors were about even. Big Bob certainly looked happier than Jack could ever remember seeing him before. Well, he had good reason for feeling light-hearted, since in a flash he had been enabled to throw overboard the terrible weight that had for days and weeks been lying upon his soul, and making life unhappy for the poor fellow.

"But, Jack," Bob went on to say, earnestly, "right now I want you to understand that I mean to profit by this thing."

"Yes, I remember you vowed you would, Bob," remarked the pleased captain of the Chester eleven, once more easy in his mind, and no longer seeing that horrible gaping weak spot in the line-up.

"This is going to be a lesson to me," continued Bob, soberly. "I've turned over a new leaf for keeps. Just let me catch myself acting careless again, whether in small things or in weighty ones, that's all. If I do I'm resolved to punish myself severely. That fault has *got* to be conquered, once and for all."

"Fine for you, Bob," Jack told him. "And so in the end the terrible trouble that threatened to break you all up, and keep you from enjoying the sports you love so well, has turned out to be only the best thing that could ever have happened to a fellow with a bad fault. That's the way things often go, Bob. Every fellow can look back and see a number of happenings that at the time he considered to be almost calamities; but long after they are past he discovers that they only forced him to change his calculations, much to his profit in many ways; so that they turned out to be mere stepping-stones on the road to success."

"Well," the other went on, "I just couldn't keep the good news from you, Jack, so I ran over to tell, because you've been such a great help to me in my time of trouble. And, Jack, there's something more. Tonight, after the game's all over, I've made up my mind I'm going to have a good heart-to-heart talk with my father."

"Yes, I think that would be a wise move for you, Bob," said Jack, deeply impressed.

"I want him to know first of all what it was worried me all this while; that instead of my being sick in body I was sick at heart, and grieving because I had, as I feared, done him a great wrong. Yes, I'm going to tell him everything, even to how we put that paper where he could see it, so he might take a notion to write a second and a third letter, and make dead sure. He must know that I've changed, and had my lesson that will make me a different sort of a fellow. Besides, my dad has changed, too, as you know; and I firmly believe that after this we're going to be regular chums."

"It couldn't be better, Bob, and I certainly congratulate you on the way things have come out. And of course, after such a glorious piece of news striking you on this particular morning, you'll be able to eat your Thanksgiving turkey and pumpkin pie with the right sort of spirit."

"Will I?" laughed the fullback; "well, they'll wonder whether there's any bottom to my stomach today, for I've got a lot of neglected dinners to make up for, you know. The sky never did look one-half so bright to me as this morning, after I learned the great news. It would seem cheery even if black clouds sailed over, and the snow began to fritter down; because my heart is as light as a feather right now, and there's no place for gloom down there."

"I'm glad in many ways that this has happened just now," continued Jack. "First, I'm glad on your account, because you certainly have had a rocky time of it for long dreary weeks. Then I'm rejoiced for your father, because he has such a true-blue son, and has only just found it out. Last of all, I'm feeling particularly joyful for the sake of Chester, because after this, Bob, I expect you'll be in trim to play the game of your life this morning against Harmony Tigers."

"Just you watch my smoke, that's all, Jack. Why, I feel as if I could do almost anything, I'm that full of ginger and snap and happiness. The cobwebs have all been swept clear from my brain, and Robert is himself again. If I don't do Chester credit today just take my head for a football, and boot it, that's what. But I must be going now, because both of us have things to do before we dress to go out on the field. This will be a banner day for the old town. It's been a long time back since they've seen a genuine game of football here. I'm glad you drew the choice, because in Harmony there's always an element that tries to make it unpleasant for visiting teams, none of which is found in Marshall or in Chester, where we treat our visitors as true sports-men should. Well, so-long, Jack. I couldn't keep such good news any longer, you understand."

"And I'm mighty glad you didn't, Big Bob; for you've given me a whole lot to be thankful over. When I heard some one wanted me at the 'phone I was conjuring up all sorts of evil things happening that would threaten our line-up. Even after I heard your voice I wasn't at all sure but you meant to tell me your father had learned the truth, and ordered you to stay at home today. But everything has come out gilt-edged, and we can afford to laugh."

"Yes," sang out the happy Bob as he started for the door, "everything is lovely, and the goose hangs high; only today I reckon the bird will turn out to be a turkey instead. I'll be on deck long before time for the game, Jack, and something tells me we're going to give those fighters from Harmony the tussle of their lives, as well as win the game from them."

"I hope you're a true prophet, Big Bob," laughed Jack,

waving his hand after his friend, and then closing the door.

Indeed, he felt, as he said, like "shaking hands with himself," the reaction had been so great, and Bob's news so satisfactory. It might be looked at as an omen of good luck for the momentous occasion. Surely a day that had opened in such a glorious manner for Big Bob, and the team in general, could not have bitterness and gall in store for those gallant Chester fellows who expected to improve upon their work in Marshall, and tear a victory on the gridiron from Harmony's team.

Jack occupied himself in various ways until it was time for him to sally forth and join his band at the rendezvous. Then in good time they would head for the field, where they might expect to see a perfect mob awaiting their coming.

CHAPTER XIX

LOCKING HORNS WITH HARMONY

Such a crowd had never before been seen in Chester, according to the opinion of the oldest inhabitant. The fact of its being a holiday had something to do with it, of course. Then again the recent victory of the home eleven over Marshall seemed to have electrified the entire community, which was rapidly becoming "sport mad," as some of the old fogies complained.

The Harmony Tigers showed up in a big carry-all motor-van about the time Jack and his followers trooped on the field, and began to pass the ball around to limber up their muscles for the great test. They were given a royal reception, for there were many hundreds of Harmony rooters on hand to help the boys with cheers and the waving of flags and pennants. Besides, Chester was showing a fine spirit that could applaud a clever play, even on the part of the enemy team, though naturally their best yells would be reserved for the home boys.

When the two teams lined up facing each other they stood as follows:

Chester	Position	Harmony
Jones	L.E	Osterhide

Jackman	L.T	O'Leary
McGuffey	L.G	Bailey
Griffin	Center	Chase
Hemming	R.G	Boggs
Badger	R.T	Leonard
Douglas	R.E	Clifford
Hopkins	Q.B	Martin (Capt.)
Mullane	L.H.B	Oliver
Winters (Capt.)	R.H.B	Oldsmith
Jeffries	F.B	Hutchings

Really it looked as though the Tigers outclassed their opponents at the ratio of five to six, so far as weight and brawn went. They were an even heavier aggregation than the Marshall team; which, by the way, had been snowed under on the preceding Saturday to the tune of 27 to 6, the Harmony boys scoring almost at will; and this sort of proceeding of course warned the whole Chester team, watching eagerly from the side lines, what they would be up against when their day came.

The game was started, and it was a seesaw affair all through the first period, play being kept near mid-field most of the time, with the advantage on neither side. Consequently, when after a brief intermission to allow of any necessary changes in the formation of the teams, not required as yet, the crowd was unable to decide where the advantage lay. But Harmony fans kept saying that the time had not yet come for their favorites to break loose; when it did there would be "something doing" to make Chester folks "sit up and take notice."

This proved to be poor prediction so far as the second

quarter went. Indeed, the tide started immediately to set in the other direction. Hopkins, quarterback for Chester, scored a touchdown in this period that carried the crowd off its feet with excitement, it was so cleverly done. He took a forward pass from Winters, who shot the ball from the fourteen-yard line zone.

The defense of Harmony was all set and ready, but the artful Hopkins must have discovered a small opening through which he managed to dash. It was, taken altogether, a daring play, and succeeded as much from that reason as anything else. In football the unexpected counts most, and Harmony was certainly caught napping.

Winters made his difficult pass as swift and sure as a rifleshot into Hopkins' arms. In a moment the Harmony backs downed him, but the tackle came too late to save the score.

This touchdown really had its origin in an error of the Harmony team - just one of the errors that add thrills to the enjoyment of the crowd, but which must have doubtless made the respective coaches shudder. Chester kicked off at the beginning of the second half, and Captain Martin of Harmony ran the ball back to the 39-yard line, where he was tackled so hard by Jones that he fumbled, and Badger fell on the ball for Chester.

The Harmony team was thrown into momentary confusion by this sudden turn in affairs, and Chester was quick to take advantage of the opportunity thus thrust upon them. On the very next play Winters called for an end-over play which left Jackman clear and alone; and accordingly Badger heaved a pass to

Jackman, who dashed to Harmony's 20-yard line before he was dragged down.

A thrust at the line was repelled, but another pass, Winters to Griffin, gained 5 yards, and the ball rested on Harmony's 5-yard line. An attack on Harmony's line resulted in a 3-yard loss, and on the last down Winters resorted to the play that resulted so advantageously for his side.

The ball traveled through a charmed zone, it seemed, for a dozen Harmony hands leaped out to bat it as it sped along into the arms of the Chester quarterback.

Thus at the beginning of play in the third period, after Harmony had brought two new men into the field, and Douglas, for Chester, who had been injured, was replaced by Wiggins, the scare stood 6 to 0 in favor of Chester, for of course it had been easily possible to kick a goal following the touchdown.

Harmony looked dangerous at once. They started in as though determined to make amends for that blunder which had cost them so dearly.

Those in the grand-stand who knew the signs best settled back with the comfortable feeling that Harmony had at last awakened to the fact that with half the game over they were in peril of being beaten, which would cover them with shame. It was bad enough to have lost to Chester in baseball, but to have to yield the supremacy of the gridiron to the same town would be a calamity indeed.

So they just tore their way down the field, and soon had Chester fighting madly to keep them from a touchdown. There was some really brilliant play shown here, on both sides, that called forth frenzied cheers. But the applause died away like magic almost as quickly as it started; for everybody knew how essential it was in a grim struggle like this that the players should be allowed to hear the signals called out by their leaders.

The hilarity of the Harmony rooters increased when Oldsmith, right halfback, crashed through left tackle for a gain of 8 yards, dragging a couple of Chester tacklers with him. Hutchings plunged straight ahead for 6 yards more, and the ball was then on Chester's 8-yard line.

There began to arise a howl for a touchdown as the Chester players braced themselves for the shock. The Harmony line shifted quickly and a double pass was tried. Martin tossed the ball to Hutchings, who shot it toward Oldsmith for a dash upon Chester's 6-yard line. Oldsmith reached the ball, but it slipped through his eager fingers, and was buried under a swirl of Chester fellows.

After that the Harmony team waxed anxious again. They had learned that this Chester aggregation was all that Marshall had found it to be, if not more so. Their line tightened up at the critical places, and their right halfback, Oldsmith, proved himself to be a very dangerous person, likely to circle the ends, and break up the game at any stage.

Soon another drive was started on the part of Harmony, seemingly determined not to be denied the touchdown so urgently needed. Sheer weight carried Chester back, as it seemed, helplessly. Plainly the only way to counteract this advantage on the part of Harmony was through cleverness and swiftness. Captain Winters unbottled another of the tricks which old Joe Hooker had taught them, and the crowd gasped in wonder as they saw the tide again turn in Chester's favor, since they had possession of the ball.

Back and forth the battle raged. It was furious while it lasted, and kept everybody keyed up to top-notch excitement. Most of the fighting in this period was done on Chester territory, however, for despite their utmost endeavors Jack and his boys seemed unable to carry the war into the enemy's country.

With but a short two minutes to cover Harmony finally took a mad pace and managed to get the touchdown so ardently desired, as well as a subsequent goal, making the score a tie, just as it had been at the end of the third period when Chester and Marshall locked horns.

The mighty Harmony machine-roller seemed at fault when trying to crush all opposition on the part of Chester. Something seemed to have happened - either Harmony was weaker than when playing last with Marshall, or else they found the defensive tactics of their latest enemy more stubborn and resourceful.

The last quarter opened, and again the fight raged bitterly. Jack uncorked more of the contents of the trick bottle, and as a result the ball was over on Harmony territory from the start. Captain Winters had figured it all out, and knowing what slight chances they had of securing another touchdown against those stalwart fellows, he had determined to risk everything on a kick from placement.

Somehow he seemed to feel this was Big Bob's special day, and that some of the glory ought to be given to him in order to prove that happiness can work wonders, even on the gridiron. So with an eye on the chances, also observing the slant of the wind, and such minor yet important things, Jack tried his best to work matters that the ball would still be in their possession when on Harmony's 30-yard line.

At last he gave the signal. The crowd stood up to see better when it was realized that a kick from field was going to be resorted to. Jack himself sprawled there on the ground to grip the ball, while Jeffries poised himself to deliver the boot that might settle the whole game.

Such a play is a spectacular thing when done properly, and particularly when attended by success. With the halfback down flat and holding the oval, and the kicker with one eye on the ball and the other on the tacklers just breaking through it is not the easiest thing in the world to do. There was intense silence, so that the sound of the blow was plainly heard, even in the grandstand. Up rose the ball, describing a graceful arch. Would it fall between the goal-posts, or, carried by the wind, drop far to one side? Everybody was doubtless asking himself or herself that question.

Then it was seen to drop exactly between the posts and well beyond, really one of the most beautiful kicks ever seen. A mighty roar from the crowd attested to the admiration felt for Jeffries, the fellow capable of doing such a fine piece of work.

With the score 9 to 6 and against them Harmony now started in to make a last game fight to carry the ball across into hostile territory; but there were only four minutes left in which to do or die.

Mark Overton

CHAPTER XX

THE GREAT VICTORY - CONCLUSION

Striving like mad Captain Martin and his ten followers tried to rush the fighting, so as to get another touchdown before the referee called the game; for that would fill them with joy, since it meant the score would be reversed and stand at 12 to 9.

Just as bent on preventing such a calamity Jack and the Chester boys braced themselves to out-maneuver all attempts looking at a successful run. At times their line proved a veritable "stone wall" to the heavy Harmony halfbacks, who were dragged to earth before completing their intended long runs. Still there was a constant gain, with the ball still Harmony's. That one bitter fumble seemed to have stiffened their game wonderfully, for it was not repeated.

Time was passing, but, so, too, was Harmony creeping up. One good run now was likely to wind up the game, for Chester could never hope to retrieve such a misfortune. Visiting rooters were frenzied, and every little forward movement on the part of their team was greeted with a burst of yelling that sounded almost like the discharge of a cannon, it came so suddenly, and died out again as quickly. Oldsmith was the dangerous man, Jack well knew. Somehow he felt certain that to him had been delegated the task of carrying the ball through, and putting it over for the needed touchdown. Several times Harmony might have tried for a field goal, and the fact that they declined to accept this chance told Jack what was in the wind. They were a greedy lot. A goal from field would have netted them just 3 and tied the score, but it would also have injured their chance for making a touchdown within the prescribed time; and Harmony meant to either win that game, or lose it, with no halfway measure as a tie to carry home with them.

Well, Jack Winters was a good guesser, for just as he decided it fell to the Harmony halfback to make the attempt. The bluff was dazzling, and deceived nearly all the Chester players, so that it looked as though Oldsmith with the pigskin oval in his grip would have a clear field to the coveted place in the line where he could drop for a touchdown, and victory.

But he counted without the fleet Winters, who was after him like a shot, and determined to make his tackle before Oldsmith could cross. This of course was the real crisis of the entire game; it was win or lose for a certainty, because not a half minute of time remained, and a new attempt could not be made if this one proved futile.

Faster than the wind the two players tore along. There was no other opposition offered to Oldsmith. Indeed, the rest of the field almost stopped play, to watch the result of this duel of speed.

Oldsmith was a shade heavier than Jack. He had also been engaged in more scrimmages latterly, and might have been a bit short of breath. Such things count heavily against a player in football work, and they certainly did in this case; for it could be plainly seen that the Chester captain was overtaking the possessor of the ball, despite his most frantic efforts to keep his own ground.

Could he reach the line before being dragged down? Jack seemed inspired to abnormal efforts, as though he knew how those whom he loved were watching, and hoping, and feeling confidence in him. Once before in the game with Marshall he had been called upon to win for his team by a supreme effort; that time it was in the way of offense, whereas now it seemed to be along the line of defense. But no matter, one was just as important under certain conditions as the other.

Jack overtook his man, and made a beautiful tackle, bringing Oldsmith to the ground just in time to prevent him from scoring his touchdown. It was a thrilling moment when this occurred. The vast crowd remained silent for a second, as though hardly able to grasp the truth that Harmony had shot her last bolt and lost. Then came the din of cheers that soared to the very clouds, it seemed, such was their intensity. Confusion reigned, with a whirling mass of Chester boys dancing around and hugging each other, while the faithful girl rooters broke out into frantic shrieks, waving their beloved school colors in riotous profusion.

Of course Harmony tried to rally in the brief space of time yet remaining, but by now the Chester team was sure of its ground, and backed Captain Winters up handsomely; so that when presently the referee blew his whistle nothing had been accomplished.

So the great Thanksgiving game ended in favor of

Chester. It would be the last battle on the gridiron for that season, as is customary. The boys gave Harmony a salvo of cheers to try to take some of the bitterness of the sting of defeat away, but doubtless Captain Martin and his squad felt pretty sore to be beaten at the hands of these newcomers in the game.

Martin was man enough, however, to shake hands cordially with Jack, and tell him that he certainly had a clever team back of him. Of course, like most Harmony fellows, he believed the hard knocks of the game had gone against their side, and that if the "luck" had been more evenly distributed they would surely have won; but then all that sort of talk invariably follows when a team wends its way back home after getting "licked." There seems to be some sort of consolation about figuring out just what share luck had in bringing about disaster.

There was no mad celebration that night, as on the occasion of the victory over Marshall. The town authorities had forbidden a single bonfire to be started in the streets of the town. That burning of the Adkins home must serve as a lesson, through which they should profit. Instead, a banquet was arranged for an a succeeding evening, by some of the friends and admirers of the football team, which all the boys, substitutes as well as regulars, should be invited to attend, and at which speeches would be in order. There would also be a little statement from the head of the financial committee connected with the gymnasium then building, telling just what progress had been made, and how every dollar of the expected expense had been guaranteed, thanks mainly to the generosity of their esteemed fellow citizen, Mr. Philip Adkins.

Chester was now well started on her career of outdoor sports. Other towns less fortunate envied her the possession of that splendid gymnasium where, during the long winter evenings, basket-ball could be played, and all sorts of athletics indulged in under a competent instructor. There could be no doubt that it would prove of inestimable benefit to the growing lads, not only serving to keep them off the street corners at night, but also enable them to strengthen their bodies, and enjoy fellowship with their mates under uplifting conditions.

Big Bob carried out his scheme as mentioned to Jack and on the very morning after Thanksgiving he took pains to let the other know the result. His father had heard the whole story with deepest interest, and then told Bob that he was very glad such a thing happened, since it had really been the means of taking the scales from both their eyes, and allowing them properly to appreciate one another.

Bob assured Jack that his father was a different man nowadays, and showed an increasing appreciation for healthy sports, and the welfare of boys in general.

Although the football season wound up with that glorious Thanksgiving victory, it must not be assumed that there would be any lack of fun abroad in Chester, with the coming of the time of snow and ice. With that magnificent sheet of water at the door of the town, in the shape of Lake Constance; also the crooked Paradise River beckoning the boys to explore its upper reaches, and the mysteries to be found there, surely winter should open up a new round of exciting outdoor activities for Jack and his friends. That this proved to be the case is evident from the title of the next story in the Series, which it is to be hoped every reader of this volume will secure and enjoy to the full - "Jack Winters' Iceboat Wonder; or, Leading the Hockey Seven to Victory."

Mark Overton